Shep wagged his tail and sniffed at his leash on the table. "I'm ready to Go," he whimpered.

"Sorry, Shep." The boy tousled Shep's fur, then picked up his bag. "No dogs allowed." He followed the woman out of the den.

The door closed and Shep heard a click. He stood near the door and listened to the footsteps of his humans. He heard their steps echo in the stairwell, then nothing. They had left him.

# DOGS OF THE DROWNED CITY

# DOGS OF THE DROWNED CITY

# THE STORM

## DOGS OF THE DROWNED CITY

BY DAYNA LORENTZ

SCHOLASTIC INC.

NEW YORK TORONTO LONDON AUCKLAND
SYDNEY MEXICO CITY NEW DELHI HONG KONG

Text copyright © 2011 by Dayna Lorentz
Illustrations copyright © 2011 by Scholastic Inc.

ISBN 978-0-545-27643-6

12 11 10 9 8 7 6 5 4 3 2     11 12 13 14 15 16/0

Printed in the U.S.A.   40
First printing, September 2011

TO MY PACKMATES
JASON, EVELYN,
PETER, KERRY & OSCAR

# ACKNOWLEDGMENTS

Many thanks to my early readers: Kaitlyn and Amanda Johson, Angela LaCour, and Hallie-Blair Quatro; Anne Cunningham, Jennifer Decker, Shala Erlich, Mary Beth McNulty, and Matthew Weiner; and Tui Sutherland, who is so much more than just my writing guru. Thank you to my editor, Amanda Maciel, who made everything better. I feel blessed to have such a supportive family, and especially want to thank my mom, Chris Kaufman, for reading every draft. Finally, thank you to my wonderful husband for being the man of my dreams, and my goat girl for being perfection personified.

# CHAPTER 1
## A DOG AND HIS BOY

The lights over Shep were the lights of the fight cage, a white glare that blinded him if he looked up from the battle. In front of him were yellowed fangs, slashing claws, savage black eyes. This was no mere fight dog: Shep was fighting the Black Dog himself. The scents — of slobber, of lifeblood, of the Black Dog's wrath — were overwhelming. Shep tried to block the blows of the Black Dog, but he couldn't lift his legs. His paws were like stones. The men around him hollered; the other fight dogs yelped and growled in fear. Then the sand of the floor began to suck Shep down. He struggled against the pull of the sand and snapped his jaws at the Black Dog's snout.

A kind voice broke into Shep's suffering. He felt a hand stroke his fur. The nightmare scene vanished.

Shep opened his eyes and saw his boy kneeling before him. The boy smiled and patted Shep's head. He said something in a soothing voice. The glow of the small wall-light dimly lit the boy's face. Shep raised his head and licked the boy's cheek to reassure him. The boy seemed comforted and retreated to his bed. Shep rose and followed, making sure that his boy was safe under the covers.

"Good night, Shep."

*Good night, Boy*, Shep thought. He liked the name the boy had given him: German Shepherd, shortened to Shep. Many moons ago, in the fight kennel, he'd been just another young pup. There were only young pups and old timers in the kennel; no fight dog ever wished to know more about a potential opponent, and there were no boys to give them names or take them home at night.

Shep returned to his bed on the floor by the wall-light. He pawed at the stuffing, breaking up a lumpy section. Then he stepped into the bed, circled around a few times, and finally curled his rump under him and flopped onto his chest. His fluffy black tail tickled his nose, so he shifted his long black muzzle to the other side of his paws.

By the smell of it, there were still many heartbeats before the tails of dawn wagged in the sky. To fall back asleep was to relive the past, and Shep did not want to see that place again. He dragged a toy out from under a box and gnawed on it to stay awake.

Every night, Shep closed his eyes and hoped that the nightmare of the fight cage had been washed from his memory. But sure as the moon shined, the grisly dreams invaded his slumber and the stale stench of the Black Dog, that raging specter, filled his nose, choking him. The scars in his memory were as permanent as the scars on his snout.

But that was all in the past. For twelve moons, nearly a cycle, Shep had lived in a good den with a kind boy and his kin, a tall man with a furry face and a plump woman with long, silky black hair. The boy, lanky with shaggy brown hair, was Shep's favorite. He was the one who rolled around on the rug with Shep, tugging on a rope toy. The boy was the one who took Shep to the Park every morning and played fetch with the yellow Ball. The man and the woman were nice enough, but Shep loved the boy best.

The boy twitched in his sleep and made a soft groaning noise, then snored on. Shep nibbled an itch on one of his front paws, licked the fur to straighten any wayward brown hairs, and laid his head down. He was far from the fight cage, and he was happy.

The morning sunlight glinted off the buildings outside the room's window. Shep was hungry. He crept over to the boy's bed and, in a single spring, was on top of the boy and licking his face. The boy laughed as he fought off Shep's gentle attack.

"Okay, okay," he said, shoving Shep's snout playfully. Then he said something about the Park.

*The Park!* His hunger forgotten, Shep jumped down from the bed. The boy yawned, his ripe breath smelling of happy dreams, and crossed the hall into the Bath room.

Shep followed the boy and stuck his snout in the door. "Let's Go to the Park now!"

"No dogs allowed," the boy said, playfully swatting Shep's nose before closing the door behind him.

Shep listened to the water rush and gurgle, knowing that it would only be a few more heartbeats of waiting until the boy appeared. The door whined, and the boy was before him. Shep stood and wagged his tail. "Can we Go to the Park now?" he yipped.

The boy slapped his thighs. "Let's Go!" he cried, and ran down the hall toward the den's entry.

Shep sprang after him, catching the boy just as he rounded the corner. "I got you!" Shep barked, pawing at the boy's chest. He clawed the boy's shoulders trying to lick his face, which reeked of mint.

Laughing, the boy stumbled into a table. The woman stepped out of the food room, face scrunched. She scolded the boy, but then she smiled, so Shep knew everything was all right. He wagged his tail at her to wish her a good morning. She gave Shep a quick scratch behind the ears.

"Come on, Shep," the boy said. He lifted the leash from its hook.

Shep was instantly pressed against the boy's thigh, nose to the door. The boy clipped the leash onto Shep's collar and led Shep out of the den, into the hallway, and down the steps.

Outside, the usual scents and sounds of the city surrounded Shep — the honk and stink of the Cars, the whistle of wind between the buildings, the tar smell of the street. But there was something else, a vibration in his whiskers and a new scent. The air was heavy with water, the breeze swirled, and energy crackled through the sky — all far away.

The boy tugged on the leash. Shep pushed the strange smell from his mind. It was a distant scent, the sky above was clear, and he was so close to the Park.

Shep and his boy bounded down the Sidewalk. Though Shep preferred roaming the whole of the street (sniffing the gutters, chasing the Cars), the boy always tugged the leash tight, forcing Shep to remain on the crowded raised stone way next to the buildings, or "Sidewalk," as the boy repeatedly commanded.

When the boy stopped across the street from the Park, Shep strained against the leash. The smells of moist dirt and rustling leaves, the wet sparkle of the water in the pond, and the dogs — so many dogs! — all pricked at Shep's nostrils. The roadway was crowded with the humans' growling, smoke-belching Cars. Shep barked at them to get out of the way.

"I have to get to the Park!" he cried.

The boy suddenly loosened the leash and they ran across the street, into the Park, and to the fenced-in area where the other dogs scampered on the grass. Shep pressed his nose to the fence and, once the boy lifted the latch, shoved open the gate.

"Run, Shep!" the boy shouted.

Shep felt the leash fall from his collar. He burst forward, springing off his hind legs. As he ran, the gusty wind ruffled his fur. His tongue lolled from his open mouth and his paws pounded the dirt.

The fenced-in part of the Park was not large. There were open stretches of grass, some trees and bushes, a bench here and there, a water hose which made terrific mud pools, and, in the center, an arrangement of obstacles — a tunnel, a platform, lines of sticks thrusting up from the earth. Shep circled around it like a flash of brown fur and returned to his boy. The boy held up the yellow Ball and Shep leapt for it.

"Sit!" the boy commanded.

Shep sat, his heart racing. He panted hard, but kept still, waiting for what he knew came next. The boy swung back his arm and threw the Ball. It flew in a high arc against the sky.

"Go get it!" the boy shouted.

Shep sprinted after the Ball, his claws flinging dirt behind him as he ran. He followed the yellow dot as it fell, his eyes flicking from Ball to grass to Ball again. At just the right heartbeat, when the Ball was only two stretches from the ground, Shep turned and sprang into the air. He clenched his teeth around the yellow fuzz of the Ball and landed on his paws.

"Another perfect catch!" Shep growled happily through clenched jaws. He trotted back to his boy and dropped the Ball at his feet.

The boy threw the Ball again and again. *This is what a dog's life should be*, Shep thought as he raced after the Ball for a fifth time. *Nothing but sky above and the wind in your fur and grass under your paws and a boy to play with.*

After a few more chases, Shep could tell that his boy was getting tired of the game. The boy's arms drooped and his throws were weak. When the boy tossed the Ball a short distance away in the grass, Shep trotted past it toward the fence. His boy relaxed his shoulders and turned to talk to another boy. Shep whimpered softly, sad to see the game end. But he wanted his boy to enjoy the morning, too.

Shep sniffed along the fence's edge to see if he knew any of the other dogs in the Park. A tall dog with a mottled brown coat bounded toward him.

"Zeus!" Shep yowled, happy to see his friend.

Zeus's pointy, cropped ears stood off his head like furry horns, and his eyes smiled beneath a proud jutting brow. He reared on his hind legs, boxing at Shep playfully with his front paws. Shep leapt up, pawing at his friend's broad white chest and nipping lightly at his jowls.

Zeus dropped onto the dirt and raised his rump in the air. He wagged his stub of a tail and gave a few quick barks. "Catch me!" he cried, then burst away across the Park.

Shep growled and took off after Zeus. He caught up with him and nipped at his flank. Zeus spun around, catching Shep's ruff lightly in his teeth, and the two rolled in the dust. They kicked at each other's bellies, open mouths gnawing at the other's neck, and growled happily.

Shep thrust his hind legs into Zeus's belly, then sprang onto his paws.

"You're too slow this morning!" Shep barked. He dug his front claws into the grass and charged through a hedge.

Zeus growled and in one twisting leap was on his paws and racing after Shep.

Shep veered around a tree and headed for the obstacle course. He ducked his head and scrambled through the tunnel. Just as he emerged, Zeus pounced from above and brought Shep down into the dirt.

Shep struggled to his paws. He looked back at the tunnel. "How'd you do that?" he asked, shaking the dust from his coat.

Zeus cocked his head toward the climbing platform. "Up the ramp, and then off the platform, and onto your head."

Shep was impressed. "Good move," he snarled.

"Well, you're older, so you have an excuse," Zeus yipped jokingly.

"Older, but wiser," Shep barked. He snapped at Zeus's stub tail, then raced off across the field. Zeus howled and took off after Shep.

Other dogs — a brown, short-haired hunting dog, a shaggy golden retriever, a black-and-white mutt — tried to break into their play, chasing first Zeus, then Shep, but the two friends ignored them. Zeus was like Shep's kin, the littermate he'd never known. When they played, Shep sensed Zeus's movements as if they were his own. He knew how far they could take a scuffle without turning it into a fight.

Several more rounds and both Shep and Zeus were panting hard. They decided to take a break to catch their breath and trotted to the shade of a tree. Some of the other dogs continued the chase, the black-and-white mutt in the lead, then the brown dog. Zeus sat beside Shep, tongue lolling between his jaws.

"This is the life, isn't it?" yipped Shep. He could

imagine nothing more perfect than this morning: his boy nearby, his friend beside him, winds rustling the palm fronds above.

"It's okay," Zeus grunted, sniffing his hind flank, then nibbling at an itch.

*"Okay?"* Shep asked, surprised by his friend's indifference. "What could be better than this?"

Zeus looked around, his gaze stopping at nothing, taking everything in with equal disdain. "I'm not sure," he said finally. "But there has to be something better than this. Don't you get bored sometimes, chasing that Ball, eating that dry kibble?"

Shep closed his eyes and recalled the horrible excitement of the fight kennels — claws rattling metal cages, endless barking and howling, raw meat thrown into the battle to intensify the fighters' fury.

"Sometimes boring is good," Shep woofed quietly.

A stout, black, smush-snouted little dog with tall, winglike ears — nearly as big as Shep's own — pranced over to where Zeus and Shep sat. He growled and then barked at them. "Think you're so big!" he yowled. "I can take you! Both of you!" He pounced on the dirt, front legs stiff and chest puffed. "Come on! You scared?"

Zeus looked at Shep, and they both burst out panting. They stood and walked away from the snorty thing.

"They're not even dogs, those little yappers," Zeus said, a wide grin on his jowls.

Shep panted and glanced back at the tree. The black yapper glowered, his tiny jaw clenched and fat chest thrust forward. He lifted his stumpy leg and marked the tree.

"It's mine now!" the yapper barked, kicking with his hind legs and sending up a spray of dust. "From now on you'll have to fight me to sit here!"

"Great Wolf!" Shep yipped, rolling his eyes. This squat yapper was ridiculous. Normally, the little dogs stayed in one corner of the Park, a separate, smaller section fenced off for the midget mongrels. Most little dogs knew their place, and that it wasn't with the big dogs. What was this crazy yapper thinking, trying to play with the real dogs?

Zeus barked that he wanted to rejoin the chase and bounded after the passing pack. Just as Shep was about to follow, he heard a growl behind him.

"You look worthy."

A large black girldog with a shock of brown fur over each of her sharp eyes padded toward him. She held her curved tail high and her stance was proud. She carried no human scent — she smelled of slobber and tar and scavenged meat. Shep could see the Black Dog smiling from behind this girldog's brown eyes.

"Wild dogs aren't allowed in the Park," Shep growled, his hackles raised.

The girldog cocked her head. "Are you going to make me leave?" she snarled.

"If I have to," Shep replied coolly.

The girldog snickered, then sprang at Shep. Her attack was ferocious, and her teeth snapped savagely. She caught Shep's ear with her fangs.

Shep yelped as he felt his flesh tear. The pain brought him instantly back to the fight cage. He slashed at the girldog as he had at every other opponent he'd faced. His claws raked across her nose.

The girldog squealed and lunged to the side. She licked her nose, tasting the lifeblood.

"You *are* worthy," she grunted.

Shep growled, his teeth bared, his jowls trembling. Her flank was exposed, muscles tensed on her outside leg. Her next attack would be high; he would lock his teeth on her scruff from below, and roll her into the dirt.

But the girldog loped away from him. She sprang off a bench and hurdled over the fence.

"If you're ever interested in being wild," she bellowed, a mean smirk on her snout, "just howl for Kaz." She bounded away into the unfenced area of the Park.

Shep's muscles tensed, ready to give chase. He snorted and shook his head, trying to clear the fight from his mind. Just a few heartbeats of real fighting, and he was drowning in the scent of lifeblood, blinded by the lights, deafened by the barks and shrieks and howls —

"Shep!"

His boy ran to his side and knelt by his head. The boy said something in a worried voice and held aside the fur from the tear in Shep's ear. The boy took a corner of his shirt and dabbed at the scratch.

His boy's voice and soft touch brought Shep back to himself; he was deeply grateful. He ducked his head away. "It's nothing, Boy," he whimpered, licking the boy's hand.

*I am far from the fight cage*, he reminded himself. *I am with my boy.*

A strong breeze ruffled Shep's mane. Thick gray clouds were rolling over the Park from sunset, carrying with them the strange scent Shep had picked up earlier. A light rain began to fall.

"Breakfast?" the boy asked, glancing at the menacing sky.

Shep barked and wagged his tail. He followed his boy across the grass, out of the Park, and home to the safety of their den.

# CHAPTER 2
## LEFT BEHIND

Shep's family's den was in one of the older-smelling buildings on the block. Some buildings were painted bright colors and stank of fresh-cut wood and varnish; others were new, made of metal and glass, and reeked of sour chemicals. But Shep's building smelled of humans, of their sweaty shoes and spicy food — it was as if each brick bore the scents of all the people who'd made their dens in the building over the cycles. Every time Shep pressed his snout to the metal door of the building's entry and scented those friendly smells, he barked a quick woof of thanks to the Great Wolf for guiding him to such a perfect home.

As Shep and his boy climbed the last few steps to their den, Shep smelled a stranger. Sure enough, an unknown, dark-skinned man in a white shirt stood outside the entry door talking to the boy's kin. The man held a board with papers stuck to it. Shep sniffed: The man did not smell dangerous, but the boy's kin were extremely anxious.

Shep growled a warning: "I protect this den."

The white-shirted stranger stopped talking, turned, and pointed at Shep. "No dogs allowed," he said.

Shep snarled. This man was not from Shep's family; he had no right to give commands. But the boy's kin seemed cowed by this man in the white shirt. Shep's man replied quietly. He waved the woman, the boy, and Shep into the den, but remained at the door.

Shep looked up at his man as he passed and wagged his tail. His man ignored him and shouted something into the den in a commanding voice.

Shep licked the man's hand. *Did I do something bad?*

The man glanced down at Shep, patted his head, and returned his attention to the stranger in the white shirt.

Shep padded into the main room of the den. The floor-sucker lay dead on the rug, its long, tubular neck extended in front of its bulbous body like it'd been killed mid-suck. The woman stood next to it, her eyes fixed on the blinking light-window in the corner. The light-window showed a small man pointing at a picture. The picture had swirls of color that moved back and forth, and a little cloud that flashed with lightning. With each swirl, the woman muttered to herself. There was nothing unusual about this to Shep; often the man and woman stared at other men and women in the light-window. Shep only worried about the light-window when other dogs tried to get into the den through it. When that happened, he had to bark a warning to let the offending dog know that this den was protected.

The boy called to him from the food room and Shep scampered in. His stomach gurgled; he was hungry after playing and fighting in the Park. The boy placed Shep's bowl of kibble on the floor, but instead of sitting at the table beside Shep to eat his own kibble as he always did, the boy left the room.

*Why isn't the boy eating his kibble with me?* Shep wondered as he crunched a mouthful.

The woman came into the food room and began filling several large bowls, some with Shep's kibble and others with water. She placed them on the floor, all of them — more food than Shep had ever been fed before.

*Well, I am feeling quite hungry*, Shep thought happily. He stepped toward the food.

"No, Shep," the woman commanded.

*Why no?* wondered Shep. He sniffed the bowls to make sure that they were his kibble and not the boy's or his kin's. He'd been right the first time — the bowls were full of *his* kibble.

"No," the woman said again, wagging a finger at his snout.

The man called to her from the entry and she shooed Shep out of the food room in front of her.

Shep slunk down the hall, tail lowered. "Why can't I eat my own kibble?" he whimpered.

Shep found the boy in his room, shoving body coverings into a bag. Shep sniffed: The boy was anxious and upset. He began speaking to Shep in a worried voice. He said "Go" and "Car."

*What about Car?* Shep wondered. He waved his tail. Perhaps the boy would take him in the Car, and they could both Go somewhere, together.

The boy tugged lightly on Shep's scruff, then walked out of the room. Shep followed him, loping alongside the boy's legs. Shep loved Going in the Car. Sometimes the Car took them to the beach, where Shep could really dig his paws into the sand.

The man stood beside the entry door with several filled bags. "Be good, Shep," the man said.

The boy said something to the man, his voice angry.

Why was the boy angry? Shep pawed at the boy's bag. Why were there so many bags?

The boy knelt and hugged Shep tightly. Water fell from the boy's eyes. Why was the boy so upset? Shep whined, scared and unsure of what was happening.

"Let's Go," the woman said, coming from the back rooms. Her eyes nervously scanned the den. She said something to the boy and took his hand.

Shep wagged his tail and sniffed at his leash on the table. "I'm ready to Go," he whimpered.

"Sorry, Shep," said the boy, wiping his eyes. He tousled Shep's fur, then picked up his bag. "No dogs allowed." The woman pulled his hand and he followed her out of the den.

The man flapped open a newspaper and spread it on the mat in front of the door. He said something, patted the paper, and picked up the remaining bags. Shep tried to follow him out the door, pressing his nose against the man's leg.

"No, Shep," the man said, pushing Shep's muzzle back inside. "Stay."

The door closed and Shep heard a click. He stood near the door and listened to the footsteps of his humans. The slap of their shoes echoed in the stairwell, then nothing. His family had left him.

Shep sat by the door. This did not seem like some short break, like when the boy left with his bag full of papers, or when the woman went out and returned with kibble. There was the strangeness of the packed bags and the visit from the white-shirted man, but strangest of all, the humans had not put Shep in his crate. They always put him in his crate when they went away from the den. Did they simply forget? And what about leaving all those bowls of kibble? The humans never gave him extra kibble. Whenever he begged for more, the woman said something about fat lumps, whatever they were.

*Something strange is definitely happening,* thought Shep. *I've got to keep my nose open.*

Shep kept watch by the door for many heartbeats. He heard the patter of footsteps echoing in the stairwell — none smelled like his boy. Each time feet passed his door, he whined and scratched at the door frame. But nothing happened. The door did not open; his boy did not return.

It was midsun, but the den was dim. Shep went to the window and looked out. People carrying bags waddled, arms over heads, down the rain-soaked streets. A few Cars growled at the light below Shep's window.

When the light changed, they raced away. All moved in the same direction, the Cars and the people.

Shep glanced up at the narrow strip of sky visible between the buildings. The thick clouds he'd seen earlier covered the whole of it, moving like a flock of fat birds from sunset toward sunrise. The clouds were not unusual for this time of year, but these moved fast. The light rain continued to fall; the water glittered as it swirled in each gust of wind. Shep wished he could see more of the sky — were these clouds followed by others? He wanted to sniff the wind again — did these clouds carry more than rain? Not that it mattered to Shep: All the windows were closed and he couldn't go Outside without his boy.

The thought of Outside made Shep anxious. He needed to be walked!

Shep went to the door and sniffed the crack at the bottom. No fresh human scent reached his nose. He whined, then barked. He scratched at the door, kicking aside the newspaper the man had mysteriously laid on the floor. Shep did not want to mess inside, remembering how upset that had made the woman when he'd first arrived in the den. She had yelled at both Shep and the boy, pointing at the rug. The boy had given Shep an angry look as he scrubbed the spot with a rag.

But there was no choice. Shep had to go.

He skulked to a far corner of the living room, behind the couch. He relieved himself quickly, humiliated at having to mess when he knew it was wrong. But he couldn't wait. He would apologize to the boy and the woman when they returned. He would wag his tail and whimper and they would know he was sorry. They would have to understand.

Miserable, Shep returned to his vigil by the entry door. He curled himself into a ball, his tail covering his snout. Dim shadows stretched across the bricks of the building outside the den's windows. There was no noise from the hallway, no sound at all except the occasional whir of the cold box in the food room.

Shep's belly rumbled. He hadn't eaten in many heart-beats. He padded into the food room and stood over the large bowls of kibble set out on the shiny brown floor. Shep remembered the woman's command, that he should not eat the bowls of kibble in the food room. But he was so hungry.

Shep kept glancing at the door to the food room as he devoured his kibble. If the woman returned and caught him eating the forbidden food, she would yell at him. Worried, he ate and ate without thinking. He gobbled one bowl of kibble, then another, then another, until he'd eaten all the bowls left out by the woman. As he crunched the last few pieces, he realized what he'd done. *Great Wolf!* The woman would be horribly mad now that he had eaten *all* the kibble.

Shep's throat was parched. He lapped up some water, then scrambled out of the room and hid in his crate. Why had they left him? Shep whined and buried his nose in his paws.

Shep was asleep on the couch, which he knew angered the humans. He didn't know how he'd gotten onto the couch, but he was there and it was soft and smelled like the boy. Shep was happy. Suddenly, the cushions began to unravel. Claws raked through the stuffing, and fight dogs burst into the room like ants from a dirt pile. Shep tried to catch the dogs, to put them back into the couch. But the dogs kept coming, now from the Bath room, now from the food room, burying Shep. Shep struggled to hold the dogs back, teeth and claws in constant motion. Pictures fell from the wall. The kitchen table crashed onto its side.

Shep opened his eyes. He was still in his crate, though he'd been scratching in his sleep: His blanket was a rumpled pile beneath his hind legs. *So my nightmares have changed*, he thought.

It was night, but the sky was not black — the lights of the city shone orange and white on the thick coating of clouds. Although there were no lights on in the den, the colorful signs of the stores along the street set the room aglow. Shep stretched and went to the window. When the wind gusted, the rain splattered on the glass. He waited for many heartbeats and saw only a single Car with flashing lights roll slowly down the street.

He walked to the entry door and sniffed: nothing. Pricking his ears and holding his breath, he heard a cat mewing nearby and a dog barking somewhere below, but no human noise. He was alone. His family had abandoned him for the night. They had never left him alone at night before.

Shep had to go, and so he used the same corner to mess as before. His shame was somewhat less — the humans had left him with no other option.

Shep went into the kitchen and lapped up some water. He snuffled the bowls he'd already licked clean. Now he was hungry again and there was nothing to eat.

He sniffed at the cabinet where his kibble was kept. He pawed at the door, hooking a claw on the corner. It opened briefly before snapping shut. Shep tried again, this time careful to keep his claw on the cabinet. It opened a little farther before it snapped shut once more. After several tries, Shep got the cabinet open far enough to stick his snout into the opening. He pushed the cabinet door all the way open.

Inside, he found his bag of kibble. It fell out of the cabinet easily; only a few kibbles rattled around inside. Using his sharp teeth, he tore the bag apart and ate what remained. He was still hungry.

*There must be more food for me in here*, Shep thought. He sniffed inside the cabinet and smelled his treats. Shep pawed at all the bags in the cabinet, knocking each out to examine it. At last, he dragged out a shiny bag that smelled like his treats. Holding the bag between his paws, he used his teeth to rip it apart. The bag itself tasted terrible, but inside he found the sought-after long, thin strips of dried meat. He ate them all gleefully, slobber dripping from his jowls.

As he licked the last crumb of treat from the floor, Shep's stomach gave a low growl; he was still hungry. He nosed through the other bins and bags in the kibble cabinet, but none smelled of food. He decided to explore the rest of the food room.

The cabinets along the floor contained bowls — some metal with handles, some made of chewy plastic, some hard and clear — but no food. Shep stood on his hind legs and tried to scratch at the cabinets on the wall, but he couldn't catch his claw on their doors for long enough to swing them open.

One cabinet that he hadn't tried was the tall metal box that hummed. Shep knew that there was food in that box — he'd seen the humans open its door, felt the cool air from its insides, and smelled the kibble inside. He snuffled around the edge of the cold box's door, testing its seal with his nose. Then he scratched at the crevice between the door and the box. After a few swipes with his paw, the door opened with a sucking sound. A light shone and a cold mist wafted down. Shep sniffed the bottom shelves. Everything smelled wonderful.

At nose-height, there was a tray covered in shiny metal. Shep hooked a claw along the edge and dragged the tray onto the floor. It landed with a crash, splashing a brown liquid all over the floor and his fur. He licked it — the fresh meat and spices pranced on his tongue.

Shep lapped up the brown liquid, first from his fur, then the floor, then from inside the tray. To his delight, the tray also contained meaty morsels soaked in the brown stuff, which were so much better than that scrap of pinkish meat he'd found on the Sidewalk that one time. He had to find out what other delicious things were hidden in the box.

Shep pulled down every tray and box and bowl he could reach. They clattered to the ground, spraying bits and syrups and juices everywhere. Some tasted good, some awful. But by the end, both Shep and the floor were covered in muck.

Having emptied everything he could reach in the cold box, Shep stepped back and sat. His belly was stuffed; he panted gently. Eyelids low over his eyes, he scanned the floor. The full weight of his exploration hit him like a rolled newspaper: He had ruined the entire room. The woman would be furious!

Shep ran out of the food room and crawled inside his crate, trembling from nose to tail. Why did the boy leave him? And why for so long? If they hadn't left, Shep would never have opened the cold box and found all that yummy kibble, and he would never have gotten excited and eaten it all. He licked his paws and sulked, thinking of the trouble he would be in once his family returned.

But the humans did not return. The first tails of dawn wagged in the sky, lighting the thick coat of cloud above, and still Shep was alone in the den. Rain fell lightly onto the street below.

Shep hoped this meant that his humans could come back. The air in the den was hot and stuffy — the cold-air blower in the window was off, and all the windows shut. Shep's tongue lolled in his dry mouth. He trotted into the food room and discovered that when he'd pulled the trays from the cold box, he'd knocked over all the bowls of water that the woman had left him. He licked the empty bowls, desperate for even a drop of water, but they were dry. The floor around them was sticky with the various goos and gobbets that Shep had pulled from the cold box. There was no water anywhere!

*The Bath room*, Shep recalled. He always heard water rushing in the Bath room, and it was where he was given his Baths, which involved a lot of water. Shep scrambled down the hall. The stones of the Bath room's floor felt cool on his paw pads. He sniffed the water in the white bowl. It smelled of chemicals and flowers — and was a strange blue color. He would *not* drink that water.

Shep stood on his hind legs and licked the silver paw that stuck out of the tall white bowl; it was dry. So was the silver paw in the white tub where the boy gave him his Bath.

Shep dragged himself back the entry door and whined. He knew there was no one around to hear him, but it made him feel better to call to his boy.

*My boy will return soon*, Shep thought. *He has to.*

# CHAPTER 3
## ESCAPE

The patter of rain against the windows woke Shep. It was light out, probably near midsun, but clouds obscured the sun's rays. The rain was falling harder now than it had been at dawn and Shep heard a growl of thunder in the distance. He scented the air under the entry door — no humans had passed as he slept.

Shep stretched, first bending back, rump in the air, then forward, belly to the ground. When he looked again at the windows, there was a small brown girldog with a stunted black snout and bulging brown eyes hovering in the air Outside.

Shep raced to the nearest window. He saw that she was in fact not floating, but rather stood on the rickety metal-grate balcony that stuck out from the side of the building.

"This is not your den," he growled as a warning.

The girldog glanced at him through the window. "What?" she said, her bark strained with fear. "It was the lizard! I didn't mean to! Help!"

Shep knew her bark — for moons, he'd heard her yapping on the other side of the wall at every Car, human, or bird that dared to pass the building. She was not trying to attack his den; the yapper must have somehow escaped her own den, and now was stuck on the balcony. Her paw pads pressed through the holes of the metal grate and she licked her toes, whimpering for them to stop hurting.

"How'd you get out there?" he asked, his bark soft and friendly.

"My human left her window open," she cried, her thin legs trembling. "I saw a lizard on the grate, so I scratched my way through the screen to chase it." She looked around, forlorn. "I was so hungry — am so hungry. The lizard skittered off just as I scratched my way through. Now my paws hurt, and I'm afraid of this grate." She shivered, her short fur bristling.

"I haven't had a drink in a sun," Shep whined.

"There's water in my den," she barked. "If you help me get off this grate, I'll share my water with you."

Shep sniffed at the window. "I wish I could, but all my den's windows are closed."

"So break one," the girldog squealed, sounding desperate. Her eyes were wide with fear and she licked her jowls nervously.

"Windows break?" Shep asked. "How do you know so much about windows?"

"I like to chase things," she barked, lifting one paw off the grate, then another. "Outside things that land on the window, or near the window. Once I knocked a heavy metal thing into the glass while chasing a bug and the window broke."

Shep's family would not be happy with him for breaking a window. But he was desperate for water — what other choice did he have?

"What kinds of things break windows?" he asked.

"There," the girldog said, her nose waving toward the corner of the main room. "That light should do it."

Shep padded over to the tall light in the corner. The light was like a metal tree: It had a fat base at the bottom, then a thin stick, which stretched up to an open-mouth part that shone with light when the humans flicked a switch on the wall. Shep tapped the light with his snout; it didn't budge. The light was certainly heavy, but the glass in the window was strong — Shep had slammed his paws against it enough times to know. He wasn't sure if the girldog's plan would work, but he was so thirsty. He had to try.

Shep pushed at the tall, thin stick part of the light, first gently, then harder and harder until the whole thing began to sway on its base. With one final shove, the light toppled over and hit the nearest window with a loud crack. Now the glass looked like a spider's web.

"Push on the window with your paws," the girldog said.

Shep reared on his hind legs and pushed at the spiderweb. It gave slightly against his paws — the girldog was right! Shep pushed harder, thrusting off his hind legs.

"Watch it!" the girldog barked. "Jump from the floor and push once with your paws, then jump away. Broken glass is sharp."

Shep followed her advice, seeing as she'd been right about everything else. He leapt off his hind legs, shoved his paws into the glass, then caught the wooden edge of the window with his hind claws and thrust himself back into the room. The window splintered and fell Outside, onto the grate.

Shep stood on the couch and looked out through the hole in the window. Shards of glass glinted in the rain, sharp as fangs.

"Now what?" he growled, frustrated. All that work, and he still couldn't get out of the den.

"I don't know," the girldog yapped. "Get something to cover the sharp bits."

Shep thought about this: He needed something to protect his paws. Like shoes! The woman had put shoes on Shep's paws once, but Shep instantly pulled them off and he hadn't seen them since. And even if he could find his shoes, he couldn't put them onto his own paws. Perhaps the mat by the entry door would cover the sharp bits?

Shep ran to the entry and pulled up the mat with his teeth, knocking off the newspaper. He dragged it to the window, onto the couch, and then swung it through the hole. He had to push the mat with his snout to get it all the way through, but, once through, it flopped onto the grate and covered the clear bits completely.

"Now jump out and help me!" the girldog howled.

Shep looked at the hole in the window. Glass still hung inside the window frame like a mouth full of teeth. "Wait!" barked Shep. He had an idea.

Shep went into the Bath room and pulled up the mat that lay on the floor beside the tub. He dragged it into the main room, up onto the couch, and, gripping it firmly between his teeth, flung it out the hole in the window. It landed on the glass still clinging to the window frame.

"Did the first mat not look soft enough?" the girldog yipped sarcastically.

"No," Shep growled. "The first mat won't protect me as I climb out the window."

The girldog cocked her head, thinking, then cowered. "I should've thought of that," she whimpered.

Shep balanced on the edge of the couch, then put his forepaws on the windowsill. He leaned back, raised his paws high, and sprang off his hind legs. He cleared the window hole completely and landed on the mat-covered grate.

Shep barked with joy. "I did it!"

"Brilliant!" the girldog yipped.

Shep turned on the mat so that he could give the girldog a proper sniff. Through the wet, she smelled like humans and dirt, good dog smells. He wagged his tail and she wagged hers back.

"My name's Shep," he said.

"I'm Callie," the girldog replied. "Now let me onto that mat!"

"Sure thing," Shep yipped. He pulled the mat from the window hole and flung it onto the grate in front of him. It landed right at Callie's paws.

"Double brilliant!" she howled, leaping from the grate onto the mat. "Oh, that feels better." Callie sat and lifted her front paws, licking each in turn over and over. Her paw pads were red and swollen from being pressed through the grate.

Now that he was Outside, Shep could see the hole in the screen out of which Callie had jumped. It was far too small for him to squeeze through.

"I don't think I'm going to be able to get a drink in your den," Shep said. He lapped at the rain — the morsels of water were something, but not enough to slake his thirst.

Callie stopped licking her paws for a heartbeat. She looked at Shep, then at the hole in the window's screen. "We could scratch a bigger hole?"

Shep considered this. It would take some time to scratch a wider hole in the screen. Even then, the window itself was small and would be a tight fit for a big dog like Shep. He licked the grate, lapping up a few more drops of rainwater. "I'm so thirsty, my tongue hurts," he whined.

"We could go down — hey, there's a lizard! — to the ground," Callie suggested.

Shep looked through the grate and saw a puddle in the alley below. "Leave our dens?" He was thirsty, but was he thirsty enough to abandon his home and his boy?

Callie peeked over the edge of her mat at the ground below. "It *is* a rather long way down, isn't it?"

Her ear twitched, once, twice; on the third twitch, she attacked the floppy ear with her hind paw, scratching furiously. As quickly as she'd attacked, the itching spell was over. She stood and shook herself, nose to curly tail, then looked at Shep as if nothing had happened, as if he were the weird one.

"Well, for one thing," said Callie. "I'd like to get out of this rain — look at that black bird! So we either die alone inside our dens — and another! — or try to get into the alley." Her muzzle flicked back and forth, up and down, eyes peering this way and that.

*This little dog is one kibble short of a bowl*, thought Shep. *And who does she think she is, barking orders at me? I came out here to save her, after all.* Shep shook the rain from his fur. He was about ready to jump back through his den's window and risk death.

"There are stairs!" Callie barked.

Shep squinted through the holes of the grate. It was hard to see anything through the blur of the rain, but Shep could make out a metal staircase leading from their balcony to another just like it two stretches below.

"Perfect!" Shep woofed. They could climb back up the stairs to their dens after they got a drink! The only thing was how to get from where they sat to the top of the metal stairs.

*What would my boy do?* Shep remembered how, when he got a Bath, his boy laid towels down, end to end, leading from the Bath room down the hall to keep Shep's wet paws from sliding on the slippery floor. *I've got it!*

Shep stepped onto Callie's mat. He dragged his mat along side of them, and then in front of Callie's. The mat reached the first step.

"Super brilliant and a rawhide chewie!" yipped Callie. "Shall I go first?" Her tail wagged so violently that her whole rump waved from side to side.

"No," barked Shep. Even soaking wet, abandoned by his family, and cowering on a grate, he had pride enough not to follow a small and rather nervous yapper.

"Okay," she barked, annoyed. "But let's get a move on. I smell something delicious down there." Slobber dripped from her jowls.

They made their way down the stairs easily — the steps were solid metal and didn't hurt their paws. They dragged their mats behind them, and then placed the mats one after the other along the grate to the next set of stairs.

As they worked, Shep wondered about Callie's fascination with lizards. "You said you were hungry and went after a lizard?" he asked. "What made you think that the lizard would be good to eat?"

Callie sat on her haunches and squinted at the raindrops. "I don't know exactly," she said at last. "Something inside me just told me. 'Hungry?' it said. 'Then eat that lizard.'"

Callie trotted onto the mat in front of her and began her way down the stairs. Shep thought about all the lizards he'd ever seen — none had seemed particularly edible, covered as they were in scales and spiky bits.

"It's like with the Red Dot," Callie continued. She stopped and looked at Shep, ears pricked. "Have you seen the Red Dot?"

Shep dropped his mat. "Red Dot? Never smelled it."

The little dog sat back and stared out at the building across the way, her brown eyes wide and unfocused. "The Red Dot is crafty, oh so crafty. It's fast and tiny, so tiny it can never be caught, neither by claw nor fang.

It makes no sound and has no scent. My girl waves a metal stick to summon it. It appears out of nowhere and disappears just as mysteriously."

Shep didn't like the sound of this Red Dot. "Is it dangerous?"

The little dog snapped to her paws. "I don't know. But something inside me says, 'Chase the Red Dot!' — the same something that told me to eat that lizard." She trotted ahead, mat squeezed between her jaws.

Shep and Callie climbed down three sets of stairs. When they reached the fourth grate, there were no more stairs. Instead, this balcony had a hole that dropped straight down into the alley, which was three or four stretches below.

Callie looked over the side. "I can't jump that." She began to tremble.

"It's not far," Shep barked, trying to sound confident. In fact, he was a little nervous about how far the ground was from where they stood on the grate. Once they jumped through the hole, how would they get back onto the grate to return to their dens? What if the boy came back and Shep wasn't there to greet him? But Shep didn't want the little dog to worry. She was so nervous.

And he needed water. They would figure something out after they had gotten a drink and some kibble in their bellies.

Callie's trembling was getting worse. "After further consideration," she squealed, "I've determined that this jump is too far. It's not bad for you, but the drop looks like ten full stretches for me. I can't jump that without breaking like a dry biscuit."

Shep spotted some large, shiny black bags in the alley. He'd seen his boy jump off his bed onto bags full of dirty body coverings without getting hurt. "Maybe I can jump down, and then roll some of those bags over? They might be soft enough to land on." Shep wished that some dog would come along and pile some soft bags for *him* to jump onto. But he was the big dog here.

"All right," Callie whimpered. "I'll try it."

Shep took a deep breath — *Great Wolf, protect me.* He sprang off the grate and through the hole. He stretched his front paws and landed hard. But Shep was used to falling — he'd been thrown many times in the fight cage, and he'd had to learn how to tuck and roll. He did this now, curling his head between his front legs, rounding his shoulder, and rolling on his back. He tumbled once, then landed on his paws, all in one piece.

Amazing! Four strides down! He barked and jumped in a circle.

"Enough celebrating," Callie cried. "Some help for the starving dog?"

Panting, Shep trotted to the pile of shiny bags and began dragging the softest of them over to the hole with his teeth. Shep piled four bags together, shoving them with his paws into a tight cushion.

"There," he woofed. "Is the starving dog happy now?"

Callie peered over the edge of the hole. She was shaking so hard, the grate was trembling along with her. She licked her jowls over and over.

"You really think I can make it?" she asked, leaning back and then forward on her paws, as if preparing to jump.

"You can make it," Shep barked. He tried to sound more confident than he felt.

Callie closed her eyes and leapt from the grate with a howl. "Ayeee!" Her little legs pawed at the air, and then she disappeared into the pile of black bags. There was a loud *whump* and the bags exploded into a fountain of human trash.

"Callie!" Shep barked. The little yapper could drown!

"I'm all right!" A part of the trash pile began to shiver

and shake, and then out squeezed Callie, covered from head to tail in muck.

"Thank the Great Wolf!" Shep bounded to her side, rolled onto his back, and pawed and nipped at her neck.

Callie panted at Shep's display, but then joined in the play, nipping him back and kicking her hind legs at his belly.

Shep licked her shoulder. "Hey, you taste good."

Callie licked at the same spot. "I *am* quite tasty."

Both dogs hopped to their paws and began to dig through the trash pile, hunting for whatever had smeared itself onto Callie's fur. They never found that exact morsel, but they found plenty of other goodies to fill their bellies.

After stuffing themselves completely, Shep moved from puddle to puddle, lapping up enough water to fill a Bath.

Callie lay in a brown box near the entrance to the alley, licking her paws daintily. "So now what?" she asked.

"What do you mean?" Shep sat down beside her to get out of the rain.

"We have the whole city to ourselves," she said. "We can do anything."

Shep looked out at the street at the end of the alley. It was normally busy with Cars and humans, all noise and smog and confusion, but now the street was silent and empty. The drizzle of rain glinted in the dull light and gusts of wind pulled at the green fronds of the palm trees.

All Shep really wanted to do was climb back into his den and wait for his boy. A chilling thought occurred to Shep — if there were no people on the street here, where was his boy? Was he trapped somewhere? Did *he* need rescuing?

Callie hopped to her paws and shook herself from nose to tail. "Let's explore," she said. "I've always wondered what's in these other buildings."

Shep felt like a tug toy caught between two hounds. Part of him knew he should wait and see if his boy returned on his own, but another part thought he should go out and search for his boy in case he needed Shep's help. Still another part bristled at the thought of how it would look to this yapper if he — the big dog, the rescuer — turned tail to cower alone in his den.

"You ready?" Callie yipped, bursting with excitement.

Shep looked up at his den and whimpered. He also had no idea how to get back up there. Before he could answer, Callie bounded out of the alley and into the street.

"Off we go!" she howled.

"Wait for me!" barked Shep. He raced to catch up. Half of him was thrilled to smell what awaited him around the corner, but the other half was filled with dread. Two more stretches, and he wouldn't even be able to scent his den.

# CHAPTER 4
## ABANDONED

They'd covered several hundred stretches, raced across the street and back, and sniffed their way down two alleys, and still Shep waited to feel the friendly tug of his boy on his collar. He had to remind himself that there was no boy, no leash. His collar jingled, loose around his neck. He was free to roam where he wanted, sniff every tree. The thought made him terribly sad.

The street was different without all the people. Shep had never felt afraid Outside with his boy, but Outside had been transformed. The rain made every surface glossy; its patter and the whistle of the wind's gusts deafened all other sounds. Shep could hardly smell anything over the scent of the rain. After sniffing several doors and smelling nothing but wet, Shep gave up all hope of being able to find his boy.

Worse yet, things that he knew weren't dangerous, things he'd never thought twice about, were on the attack. A trash can — a thing that Shep thought couldn't move on its own — tumbled down the street toward him and grazed his paw, causing a sharp pain. Shep yelped as much at the hurt as at the shock of having been wounded by a lowly trash can. He felt as helpless as a pup.

Shep couldn't rely on anything, it seemed — he had to remain vigilant, suspect everything, be ready for any threat. His eyes trained over every wall and tree and box. He flinched at a bag blowing past his flank. A flapping door caused him to scuttle across the street.

Callie, on the other hand, skipped from grass clump to trash pile to metal post, sniffing and marking and yipping with delight. A paper rustled in an alley; she dove after it and tore the paper to shreds. A bird flew over the street and she chased it, leaping into the air every few stretches. Nothing scared Callie. It was as if the strangeness of the empty street brought her to life.

"My fur!" she barked. "Isn't this the best?" Her eyes sparkled and her tongue lolled from her open mouth. "No leash holding me back, no one yelling for me to

Come or Sit — ooh, shiny!" She scrabbled along the gutter after a silver strip drifting in the trickle of rain water.

"I think we should go back," Shep grumbled. "We have to find a way into our dens before nightfall." He shook his fur. If there was no chance of finding his boy, why was he out wandering in the wet? He was soaked, and the rain was falling harder with each passing heartbeat.

"Just a few more blocks," Callie begged. "Then we'll go back, okay?" She waggled her tail and nuzzled her head into his neck.

"All right," he growled playfully, nipping her ear. "Great Wolf, you're a pest."

Callie trotted ahead of him, but not too far. "What's this about a Great Wolf?" she asked. "You keep saying that. What's a wolf?"

Shep loped over to a tree and sniffed at the short fence surrounding it. "Just something I heard about as a pup," he woofed. "The Great Wolf was the leader of the dogs many cycles ago. The story goes, 'The Silver Moon looked down and saw dogs running about, tearing into one another as they might a scrap of meat. She loved dogs above all other creatures, and did not want to see them suffering alone, dog against dog. So she found a lowly pup, newly weaned, and sprinkled him with moonstuff. The moonstuff shimmered on his hide, and he grew into a mighty dog — the Great Wolf. All dogs cowered under his sparkling white mane, and all stood to listen when he howled. He asked them to join his pack so they might hunt together and live in peace, and all bellowed with joy.'" Shep wagged his tail at the memory. "At least, that's the way the old timer told it."

"I like that story." Callie sniffed the fence, then sat beside him. "What's an old timer?"

Shep explained about the fight kennel — the dim, drafty structure filled with row upon row of narrow metal-linked cages — and about the young pups and the old timers. "This one dog had been there for many moons. His muzzle was pocked with scars and he was missing an eye. He was in the cage next to mine, and he kind of looked after me. I was a scrawny pup, just weaned and taken from my litter. I had bad dreams and barely slept with all the howling and barking in the kennel. I guess he felt bad for me, and so he told me stories of this Great Wolf to help me sleep."

"That sounds nice," Callie said.

Shep stood. "It wasn't."

"Not the fight kennel, but the old timer, I mean." She scratched her ear, then licked her hind paw. "I've

50

never lived with another dog before. I was taken from my litter and given to my girl. I've lived with her all my life — there's a good smell on this post — anyway, as long as I can remember. It would have been nice to have had an old timer looking out for me."

"Well, now you have one," Shep said, cuffing her on the ear with his paw.

Callie reared and slapped his muzzle playfully. "You're no old timer."

"I feel like one sometimes." Shep sighed. "Worn out and in need of a soft bed and my boy."

"Weird," said Callie. "I feel this energy buzzing around inside me all the time. Now, running here — this is the first time I haven't felt like chewing or digging or tearing my way out of my fur."

Callie shook her coat, sending a spray of water off her back. "Squirrel!" she barked, then tore off across the street.

A blur of gray fur splashed through a puddle — that was all Shep saw. But Callie was after it like it was a Ball. As Shep watched, the fur took form: It was indeed a squirrel. How had Callie seen that?

The squirrel bolted for a tree trunk, claws scrambling to catch hold on the stone street. Callie closed in, leapt, and landed right on the squirrel's tail. Her jaws snapped closed. The squirrel shrieked.

"I've got it!" Callie's triumphant bark was muffled by squirrel fur.

While her jaws were open, the squirrel pulled its tail free and jumped onto the tree.

"Oh, no you don't!" Callie slammed the squirrel against the bark of the tree with her paws, then sliced at its head with her fangs.

Shep raced over to the battle. The little animal squealed and scratched at Callie's nose, but Callie clenched her jaws around its neck and raked its body with her claws. Shep had no idea why Callie felt the need to fight such a little animal. He'd often chased squirrels in the Park, but why fight one?

"What are you doing?" he asked, flabbergasted.

The squirrel's attacks slowed. Its body twitched a few times, then fell still. Only then did Callie loosen her jaws. The gray thing fell from her jowls onto the sodden dirt surrounding the tree.

Callie had a crazed look in her eyes, like that of a dog in the fight cage. *The Black Dog.* Shep raised his hackles; he readied for her to turn her attack on him. But then her eyes cleared, and she wagged her tail. Her tongue circled her jowls.

"My fur, that's delicious!" She sniffed the squirrel's body. "It came from the squirrel." She licked a gash in the gray fur. "Taste this!" she said, pushing the little body toward Shep.

Shep calmed himself, happy to see that the Black Dog had not taken hold of the yapper. He sniffed the squirrel's body. "It's food?" Shep asked.

"It's that voice I told you about," Callie yipped. "I saw the squirrel and the voice said, 'Chase that!' And when I caught it, the voice said, 'Bite!' so I bit. I can't believe I actually caught the thing! I've tried so many times, but there was always a leash or I was too slow. I guess the rain helped me, maybe hid my approach. But can you believe it? I caught it! And bit it! It tried to escape when I called to you, but then I *smashed* it down —" Her eyes began to glaze over again.

Shep nipped her scruff. "Stop."

Callie shook him off. "What?" She licked her shoulder.

"You were getting a little wild," Shep woofed. "Slow down," he said. "Start with that voice. It said the squirrel was food?"

"Not exactly. Well, maybe. But it is food! Taste that!" She nudged the body closer to Shep.

Shep sniffed the fur, then licked it. It tasted amazing, like the best kibble he'd ever dreamed of, like what he was meant to eat. . . .

Callie picked up the little body and trotted under an

overhang. Out of the rain, she lay down with the squirrel between her paws and began to lick it. Then she caught a piece of fur in her teeth.

"Oh, Shep! Come taste this! This part's even better!"

But Shep could not move. His stomach soured watching the little dog devour the squirrel. He knew that taste: It was lifeblood. It was inside that squirrel, and it was also inside of dogs. Shep had tasted lifeblood far too often in the fight cage — to him it *was* the taste of the fight cage. One lick, and his mind was flooded with the smell of the sand floor, the howls of the other dogs, claws and fangs slashing, the motionless body of his opponent, lifeblood spilling forth . . .

"Hey." Callie had come back over to him. She licked his nose. "You all right?"

Her ears flopped out, friendly, and her tail wagged low. She was not an opponent; he did not have to kill her to survive.

"Yes," Shep said, shaking his head. "It's just the squirrel. That stuff is lifeblood. I've tasted it before."

"In the fight cage?" Callie licked his muzzle, trying to comfort him.

Shep shivered and the memory shook off him like the water from his coat. "I don't want to taste that ever again."

"You don't have to," she woofed. "We'll find some more kibble in the trash, okay?"

Shep panted, grinning, and waved his tail. "Okay," he said. "How's your nose?" The little dog's snout was covered in scratches from the squirrel's defense.

Callie licked her muzzle. "Huh," she grunted, then licked it again. "Tastes like the squirrel." She licked her nose once, twice, then stopped, her eyes wide. "Does this mean I could *eat* me?"

Shep panted again. The little dog was serious. "I wouldn't advise it," he said.

Callie nipped Shep's neck. "Well, I don't mean *me*," she grumbled, "but dogs. Are *we* food?"

"I guess," Shep woofed. "But I don't see anything on these streets that can chase us down."

"That's right!" Callie barked. "So watch out, squirrels! Lizards, too! We're the meanest, baddest things around!"

As they continued down the street, Callie strutted like she owned the whole city, like she was a big dog, the Great Wolf himself. Shep couldn't help but pant at her tough act. He did not feel so secure himself. He hadn't wanted to scare the little dog, but there was something on these streets that was tougher than her: wild dogs. If they ran into that Kaz from the Park, they'd have real trouble on their paws.

*　　*　　*

The sky began to darken, and the rain continued to fall in sheets. Shep hadn't scented, seen, or heard a human during their whole trek. He clung to the hope that this was simply a result of the rain having washed every recent scent away, but a part of him knew that this wasn't true. There were no humans anywhere. Every building was empty and most of the lights were out. Some windows were covered with big pieces of wood, others with metal shutters. The city was abandoned.

Other creatures sensed this abandonment by the humans. Animals used to skulking around the fringes of the human world were out in the open. Long green iguanas crawled on top of sleeping Cars. Stray cats scuttled across the streets and stood in the alleys, feasting on trash. Flocks of pigeons and gulls strutted down the middle of the empty streets. These Outsiders knew that the humans were gone from their dens, and that they wouldn't be returning for some time.

Anxiety radiated from Shep's every hair and whisker. Where had his humans gone? Where was his boy? But Callie was not at all worried. She kept telling Shep that they'd scent a human around the next corner, or the next. Still, Shep couldn't shake the feeling that he might never smell his boy again, that the man and the woman had taken him somewhere far away, where Shep couldn't find him. Why would they have done such a thing?

"I think we should go back," barked Shep. The splatter of rain on the pavement had gotten so loud that Shep had to repeat himself twice before Callie even noticed he'd barked.

"Go back?" she yipped, trotting over to where Shep stood in a doorway. "But it's not even night out."

"We can't wait until dark to return home. Things we don't want to run into will be out on the street by that time."

"Like what? I haven't seen or smelled anything bigger than an iguana." Callie sniffed the air and twisted her ears, listening. "Nothing."

"Like you could hear an enemy stalking you in this rain," Shep woofed, snickering. "You couldn't even hear me barking as loud as my lungs could manage. I can't see or smell anything, and that makes me feel worse, not better. We'll have no warning of an attack."

"Attack from what?" Callie asked, annoyance creeping into her bark. "You said we're the biggest things out here."

"I lied."

Callie's eyes opened wide and her tail flattened between her legs. "Lied?" she whined, cowering. "About what? What's out here?"

"Dogs," Shep said, his bark softer. He hadn't wanted to scare the fur off the little yapper. "Wild dogs. Remember what I told you about the Great Wolf? Well, there's another legend, about the Black Dog. As my old-timer told it, he means death for any decent dog, simple as that. He doesn't care about anything except fighting. That's what a wild dog's like. I've seen them do things, bad things."

"Like what?" Callie was trembling from nose to tail now, her legs bent, her belly low to the ground.

"Things I don't want to see again, okay?" Shep barked. "So let's hightail it home before night sets in and it becomes even harder for me to smell danger."

Shep began sniffing his way back along the faint scent of their trail, hoping the rain hadn't washed it completely away. Callie pressed herself against his flank. Every few stretches, he felt her tremble. Her eyes flicked this way and that, searching the shadows for menacing wild dogs.

Shep felt bad about having scared her into submission, but they were heading home now and that made him happy. "You want to hear the legend?"

"What! Legend? Where?" Callie's teeth chattered with fear.

"It's the story of the Great Wolf and the Black Dog," Shep woofed. He figured it might calm her down. "Listen."

*The Black Dog didn't like the Great Wolf or the peace he'd created; the Black Dog had liked things the way they'd been. He thought it was the way of the dog to kill or be killed. He was chaos, a wildness that hurtled toward death, and he hungered for the Great Wolf and the end of his reign.*

*The Black Dog knew that the Great Wolf could only remain great if he commanded the respect of all dogs. He figured that the Great Wolf could only command such respect so long as he was the toughest dog. With this thought in his jaws, the Black Dog dug up a plan.*

*The Black Dog considered himself a crafty fight dog, and so he challenged the Great Wolf in front of all the other dogs. The Great Wolf had to accept the challenge or submit to the Black Dog, and the Great Wolf knew that submission would mean a return to chaos. He accepted the challenge.*

*They fought a fierce battle, but after many heartbeats, the Black Dog sensed that the Great Wolf would prevail.*

Unwilling to accept defeat, the Black Dog took a final slash at the Great Wolf's muzzle, then stole away into the shadows, ragged tail between his legs.

The Black Dog did not give up. He found other dogs, big, tough dogs, and convinced them that they could replace the Great Wolf if they defeated him. One after the other, these dogs challenged the Great Wolf, and one after the other, all were vanquished.

Still the Black Dog would not concede his failure. It occurred to him that perhaps he had gone about things all wrong. Perhaps there was no bigger or tougher dog than the Great Wolf. As he passed a litter of pups, just a few moons old, scrabbling outside their dam's den, he got an idea. Perhaps he did not need to find a bigger, tougher dog than the Great Wolf.

One of the pups was full of lifeblood, a real terror to his littermates.

"You think you're tough?" he asked the pup.

"Tougher than you," the scrapper snarled.

"Tougher than the Great Wolf?" the Black Dog growled. "A scrawny pup could never best the Great Wolf."

The pup looked up at the Great Wolf, who sat at the mouth of his den, high on the mountain above. "I can best him," the pup growled. He scrabbled his way up to the Great Wolf's den and challenged him to battle.

*    *    *

"Shep!" Callie screamed.

Shep whipped around. Tugging on Callie's scruff were the talons of a yapper-sized bird of prey. Its brown, speckled wings beat about Callie's head and tail. Callie tried to roll to get its claws out of her fur, but the bird had her firmly in its grasp.

Shep leapt and caught the bird's wing in his teeth. He wrenched the wing down and the bird screeched. Dropping Callie, it wheeled around on its free wing. It began pecking at Shep's ears and muzzle with its sharp beak and grabbing at his fur with its talons.

Shep released the wing and flung his body away from the bird's slashing claws. Then he swiped his fangs down onto the bird's head, snapping his jaws tight. Its skull crunched between his teeth and its body fell still.

Shep dropped the bird and scrambled over to Callie. She sat in a puddle, desperately trying to lick the wounds on her back.

"I was watching for dogs," she whimpered. "You never said anything about birds."

Shep licked her scruff. "I didn't know birds went after dogs," he said. "Cats, yes."

"I'm the size of some cats!" Callie snapped.

"Well, I'm sorry I didn't say anything," Shep barked back at her. "It's not like I *asked* the bird to attack you."

Callie licked her fur, stopping after every few licks to flash a withering look at Shep.

"Can we at least get out of the rain?" Shep woofed. "I can get a better sense of the injury if we're not constantly being pelted by water."

"Fine," she said. She got out of the puddle and shook herself, whimpering pathetically as her fur ruffled. "That building looks nice."

She trotted across the street to a stone building painted bright yellow with a wide cloth stretched over its entry that covered half the Sidewalk. The building had fancy white stone balconies with flowery designs for railings — nothing like the plain metal grates on Shep's building. Even the entry was fancy: A pair of tall windows stood where the door should have been.

Callie sat in front of the clear front doors and they opened with a swish. "Shep, look! We can really get out of the rain!" She scrambled into the building. As soon as she was inside, the doors slid shut.

Shep panicked. This little yapper was nothing but trouble! He raced across the street and jumped onto the door. As soon as he did, it slid open again. Shep fell onto the floor inside in a heap.

"Hello!" Callie yapped. She stood over Shep's head, her tail wagging. "It's nice and dry in here, and there's no wind."

They were in a large, cool room with a white stone floor. Opposite the sliding clear doors was a blue wall with a wooden counter in front of it. Next to the counter, in the blue wall, were two shiny silver doors. The sides of the room were open, leading to dim hallways.

The air smelled overwhelmingly of chemicals and flowers — the humans that lived there had cleaned nearly every surface of its scents. Still, Shep could tell it was an older building; the walls smelled of the many humans who'd made their dens in this place. Also, scattered around the room were plants of various sizes, which the humans had forgotten to clean. Callie walked over to a palm tree in a pot and sniffed.

"Smells like dog central," she yipped.

Shep got his paws under him and shook the water from his coat. "You seem to be feeling better."

Callie immediately sat and licked her shoulder. "It's nice to be dry, that's all." She winced and yowled miserably.

Shep panted lightly. "Fine, fine. Let me take a look at it."

Callie came over to Shep, wagging her tail low. "Does it look bad?"

Shep gave her a long lick, covering her whole scruff. "Just a little puncture. You'll be good as new by next sun." He walked over to the clear door and began pawing at the metal along the bottom. "Now it's time to go home. How do we get this open again?"

"Help!"

"What now?" Shep barked, annoyed. He had to figure out how to get this door to slide open. He had to get back to his den.

"I didn't say anything," Callie yipped. "I think there's another dog here."

"Of course there's another dog here! And I need your help!"

# CHAPTER 5
## THE KNOB

Shep and Callie followed the bark of the other dog to a door a few stretches down one of the hallways. The light on the ceiling was dim, but even in its faint glow, Shep could see that there was no window or other opening in the door.

"We're here," barked Shep. "But there's no way for us to get in to help you."

"Just open the door!" yapped the dog.

*Just what I needed*, thought Shep. *Another yapper.*

"How can we open it?" asked Callie. She sniffed the bottom of the door, then rested her head on the floor. "I can see your paws!" she barked.

"Wonderful," groaned the other dog. "You can see

the rest of me when you open the door. One of you smells like a big dog. Am I right?"

"Yes!" yipped Callie. "Shep's a big dog."

"Good," said the other dog. "Big dog — er, Shep. You need to bite the knob and turn it. Then the door will open."

*Did this yapper just call me "Big dog"?* thought Shep. *And who does he think he is, ordering me around? Does this dog want his tail bitten off?* Shep didn't have time for this, especially from a little dog. He had to get home. He had to wait for his boy.

"I'm leaving," Shep woofed to Callie.

"You can't leave!" Callie pushed out her chest and raised her ears and tail. "Where's your sense of honor? This dog needs our help." She squinted her little eyes and cocked her head. "What would the Great Wolf do?"

Shep sighed. *Why did I tell her about the Great Wolf?* "What's a knob?" he barked. "And how do you turn it?"

The little dog snorted and snuffled on the other side of the door, muttering something about ignorant mutts.

"Who're you calling an ignorant mutt?" Shep snarled.

"Oh, nothing, nothing," yapped the other dog. "Just barking to myself. Nothing at all."

They heard claws scratching on the metal of the door.

"Up there," the dog barked. "On the door. That shiny piece that sticks out. That's the knob."

*Knob*, Shep realized, was a yapper word for the metal paw that stuck out of every door. He'd seen his boy and other humans push on these paws to open doors before. He'd tried it himself back in his den, but the door never opened for him.

"I know about knobs," Shep said. "I didn't know they were called knobs, but I've seen them before. They don't work for dogs. I've pushed on a lot of knobs and the door has never opened for me."

The other dog started snorting and snuffing all over again, this time clearly growling about ignorant mutts.

"Hey," Shep grumbled, "you want help, you cut it with the ignorant mutt stuff." *Ungrateful little yapper*, thought Shep.

"Yeah, stop getting all huffy," growled Callie. "You asked *us* for help and we're trying to help you."

The other dog sighed. "Yes, yes. I'm sorry." He coughed a bit, then continued. "You don't push knobs. You turn them, then push them."

Shep shook his head. Knobs were like paws and paws didn't turn. "Turn them? How can a knob turn?"

"Turning means — Turning is where —" The dog snorted loudly. "Oh, hang it all!" There was a sound like the yapper was fighting with himself, then a loud cough, and he continued. "Excuse me. Very sorry. Just a bit frustrating, trying to explain things. You know? Perhaps you don't. Never mind." He coughed again. "The knob rotates. Yes? You understand that?"

"No." Shep was losing patience. Even the Great Wolf must have given up on *some* things.

"Fine, fine," the dog growled. "Forget turning. Just bite the knob straight on and tilt your head."

"Bite, then tilt?" Shep woofed. "Why didn't you just say so?"

Shep positioned himself directly in front of the knob, then stood on his haunches, placing his forepaws against the door. He dropped his head to the level of the knob and bit the shiny surface. His teeth slipped off it, and where they didn't slip, they hurt, but he wanted to be done with this yapper in as few heartbeats as possible, so he clenched his jaws and tilted his head. His teeth scratched along the knob, but the knob itself didn't move. Shep pressed his paws on the door to see if it'd worked, but no: The door wouldn't budge.

"Okay, yapper. I bit and tilted and still the door won't open." Shep spat, trying to get the harsh metal taste out of his mouth.

"Did the knob move or just your head?" asked the yapper.

"Just my head."

"Well, that's not going to get us anywhere," grunted the dog. "You have to tilt your head, and move the knob at the same time."

*If this little dog yaps at me one more time* . . . Shep's teeth hurt and there were flakes of something stuck on his tongue and he was more than a little disappointed that he couldn't make a knob work when it seemed that, at least at some point, the grumbly old yapper could.

*I should just drop these yappers*, he thought. *Drop everything and turn tail for home.* But why? His den would be empty like the rest of the city. Wherever his boy was, he wasn't around here. Shep had to accept that everyone he loved had abandoned him. Now, his only friends were a nervous little girldog and an annoying old yapper stuck behind a door and this horrible, splintery, bad-tasting, teeth-hurting, tongue-poking, jaw-breaking knob!

All his anger and frustration buzzed inside him like a fly against a window. He sprang at the knob and snapped his fangs around it. Jamming his forepaws into the door frame, he tugged at the knob as if it were a tug toy. He imagined his boy on the other end of it, taunting him, so close, but always pulling away. Why did the boy leave him? WHY?!

The knob turned and the door swung open, with Shep still dangling from it, and hit the yapper square on the snout.

"Oof!" yelped the dog.

Shep released the knob and collapsed onto the floor, exhausted. He'd had a long, wet, depressing sun. He needed some kibble and a nap.

The door had dropped him inside a spare, cave-like den. The floor was shiny wood, and the gray walls stretched high to the wood-slat ceiling. The food room was connected to the main room, separated by a counter lined with tall, thin-legged chairs. Everything was too clean and hard for Shep's liking.

He spotted a comfy-looking bed near a couch made of some chemical-smelling skin. Shep loped over to it and flopped his body down. The bed was too small — his head and forelegs stuck out one end, his hindquarters the other — but it was otherwise very comfortable.

"Please, make yourself at home," grumbled the little dog sarcastically. "I'm Higgins, of the Brussels griffon line, and you must be Shep. Short for German Shepherd, I presume?"

Shep flapped his tail. "The one and only."

Higgins was very small, about half Callie's size, with wiry, short brown fur on his body and an explosion of long grayish fur all over his snout. *Like my man*, Shep thought, panting. Higgins was a dog with a human hairface! He looked ridiculous!

"What are you panting about?" Higgins asked.

"Nothing," Shep said, stifling his pants. "Just happy to have finally helped you."

"Yeah, now you can stop bossing us around," Callie yipped, sniffing a narrow table next to the door.

"And might I have the pleasure of your acquaintance," Higgins yipped, "Miss, uh, pug? Mixed with, might I say, beagle?"

Callie was instantly defensive, chest out and tail stiff. "Just because I'm not a purebred doesn't mean I'm not just as good as you," she growled.

Higgins rolled over onto the floor, paws up, showing he meant no harm. "I do apologize," he moaned. "I'm merely curious. It's part of my research."

"Research?" Shep asked.

Higgins sprang to his paws, tiny tail wiggling. "Yes! Research!" he yipped. "My human researches bugs: collects them in jars, pokes them with sticks, things like that. I thought that I should study something a bit more

71

relevant: dogs. Did you know that pugs can see a stone placed right on their nose?"

"Well, if it's for research," Callie said, sounding a bit confused, "my girl always says 'Jack puggle terrier' after my name, which is Callie, by the way."

"Jack puggle terrier," Higgins snuffled, a far-off look on his muzzle. "My snout, it's a new breed."

Shep had no idea what a breed was, but it seemed to him that between this research stuff and the mystery of the Red Dot, there was something weird about being a yapper that big dogs had been spared.

"I smell another dog," barked Callie.

"That'd be Frizzle," Higgins grumbled. "A French bulldog. Laziest pup I've ever met. He doesn't normally live in this den, but my master offered to take care of him while his master is away."

"Why were you so desperate for help?" Shep asked. "This den looks comfortable enough."

Higgins sighed dramatically. "Frizzle ate all the kibble because he was, and I quote, 'starving' in the middle of the night. And now we are in fact starving, without a kibble or treat left." Higgins leapt onto the smelly skin couch and sat, looking down at both Callie and Shep.

Shep got out of the bed and began sniffing around the den. He wasn't about to let this little hairface stand over him, as if the yapper were the dominant dog in the room.

"I smell kibble," barked Shep. "Over here, in these cabinets."

Higgins leapt off the couch and stood in front of the cabinet Shep was sniffing. His flap-ears pricked forward and stumpy tail wagged ecstatically. "Yes, I smelled it as well. I've been scrabbling at the doors all sun without luck. If you can open them, I'll gladly share whatever kibble's inside."

*Share?* thought Shep. *Like this yapper could keep me from eating whatever I find.*

"Did I hear something about kibble?"

Claws clicked on the hard floor. Air snuffled through a stunted muzzle. Shep knew that voice. *Oh, Great Wolf, not that dog.*

It was the little black yapper from the other sun at the Park. His wing-ears pricked forward, his stump tail wagged, and he puffed out his chest like a pigeon wooing a mate.

"Hey, I met you in the Park!" the black dog — Frizzle — woofed. "Never got that palm tree back from me, did you?" He strutted over to Callie and began sniffing her over. "Why, hel-*lo*, gorgeous," he growled softly.

Shep waited for Callie to bite him square on the nose, but instead, she sniffed him back, tail wagging furiously. "Hello there!" she yipped excitedly, her bark cracking a bit. "That's Shep and I'm Callie."

Callie slapped her front paws on the floor, head low, rump raised, and tail in full swing. "Let's play!"

Frizzle slapped his paws. "You're on!"

The two began a ferocious little tussle on the floor, yipping and squealing and scrabbling like two pups. Both Higgins and Shep looked on, Higgins with a tired, not-again expression on his snout, while Shep was frozen in disbelief. Could Callie actually *like* that annoying little yapper?

Then again, Callie was also a yapper, under the strictest of definitions. Maybe it was a yapper thing. But Frizzle was in a different, more annoying class of yapper. Callie was a nice girldog who was helpful with breaking things and good at catching vermin. Frizzle, on the other hand, was a waste of fur with a Car-sized ego who wouldn't be able to fight his way out of a dog bed, let alone the fight cage.

Shep had to break things up. This Frizzle was no good for Callie. As her defender and rescuer, he had to get her out of there, and quick. He jammed his claws into the cabinet and scratched the door open. "There," he barked loudly. "Kibble for all."

"Finally!" howled Higgins. He dove unceremoniously into the cabinet and started tugging on the kibble bag. Seeing as Higgins was a midget and old, the bag didn't budge. Shep grabbed a corner and dragged the bag, with Higgins hanging from its side, out onto the floor.

The smell of food roused Frizzle from his play with Callie. He scrambled over to the bag and dug furiously at the packaging.

Shep put his paw on the black dog's back and shoved him aside. "Allow me," Shep growled.

"Watch it, Big Nose," Frizzle barked angrily. "I've been in my fair share of scraps. I could take you down — if I had to." He puffed his chest out even farther and kicked his little hind paws, head low and ears back.

One look and Shep knew for sure that this dog had never fought anything more than a stuffed toy in his life. His stance was all wrong — Shep could flip him with one swipe of his muzzle.

"Hey now," Callie whimpered, shoving her way between Shep and Frizzle. "Let's just eat, okay?" She looked at Shep, then at Frizzle, and gave each a lick on the nose.

Shep decided to ignore the annoying little dog's threat, for Callie's sake. And because it wouldn't have been a fair fight. He gripped the bag with his teeth and tore a gash in it, spilling kibble all over the floor. The four ate that bag, and then Shep showed them how to open the cold box. There wasn't much food in Higgins's cold box, but Shep nonetheless enjoyed exploring the various flavors of kibble inside.

Frizzle sniffed the empty tray he'd just polished off, then licked his jowls. "Now that was a meal, eh, Higgy?"

Higgins lifted his head from a bowl. His muzzle was coated in white stuff that dripped off his whiskers. "It's Higg-*ins*, pup. How many times do I have to tell you?"

"You might want to clean up your fur, Higgy," Shep woofed, panting.

Higgins ran a paw across his nose. "Good gracious," he said. He began wiping his snout with his paws and licking them clean.

A noise like a giant Car grumbled Outside. Shep loped over to the window and rested his forepaws on the ledge. The roar of the storm sent vibrations through the wall and into Shep's claws. The rain was falling so hard that the water didn't even bead up on the window; it poured down the clear surface in a single, rippling sheet. Palm trees swayed all the way to the middle of their trunks, their green fronds whipping in the wind like Shep's woman's long hair. Shep couldn't see anything in the street — no birds, no lizards. The clouds were a gray wall, like thick fur across the sky.

Then the fur of the clouds changed: It swirled and dropped like a stone to the street. The growling became a roar and Shep was shaken from the window ledge. His whiskers tingled — the air was shifting.

Suddenly, the glass in the window burst. It flew Outside with a scream into a blinding fury of cloud. All scent blew away with the window, as if the swirling cloud contained a giant floor-sucker. The cloud flashed a set of sharp fangs, then claws, razor edges whirling.

Shep scrambled back toward the food room, the wind now tugging at his skin. He clawed his way around the wooden counter and found the three yappers cowering inside the kibble cabinet. Shep shoved his head inside, crouching in front of the cabinet and on top of the yappers, as if the dark could protect him. The four dogs trembled and the den seemed to tremble right along with them.

# CHAPTER 6
## RESCUE OPERATION NO. 2

The roar quieted to a growl, then to nothing. After a few heartbeats, all that remained was the whistle of the wind and the slap of rain on the floor under where there'd once been a window. It took several more heartbeats before the dogs crept out of the safety of the cabinet.

"I've never smelled anything like that," Callie whimpered. "Was it a wild dog, Shep?"

A tremble ran over his fur and whiskers. "No," he woofed. He did not tell her his suspicion about the monstrous wind — that it was the Black Dog, and that it was coming for him.

"What was that?" barked Frizzle. His wing-ears twitched on his fat head.

"Nothing," grumbled Higgins. "The storm. It'll be over by morning. I'm going to the bed room to get some sleep." He snorted loudly and scrabbled down the hall.

"No," snapped Frizzle. "I heard a bark."

"I just heard it!" Callie raced into the bed room and Frizzle bounded after her.

Shep stayed where he was, claws clinging to the floor. He strained his ears and scented the air. Had it been the Black Dog? Where had the windstorm gone?

"Shep, come listen!" Callie cried from the bed room.

Shep shook his head. There was only the noise of the storm, only the scent of rain. Whatever that terrible wind had been, it had vanished. Shep shivered and stretched. He wanted to curl up in the cabinet until the end of the storm, then find his boy and go home. But he was the big dog in the den. He'd better check things out.

Shep loped down the short hall into the dark bed room. There was a small window, but it was blocked by something. The shadowy forms of Callie and Frizzle stood on the large bed in the middle of the space; Shep smelled Higgins in the opposite corner of the bed.

"What?" Shep grunted. Then he heard the barking. It was muffled — he couldn't make out anything about the other dog, or what it was trying to say — but there was definitely a dog on the other side of the wall, a dog in trouble.

"We should go help him," said Callie.

"Yeah!" howled Frizzle. "I'm ready for some action."

"What if that monster wind is in there?" whined Higgins.

"Even more reason to help!" barked Callie. "Shep, let's go."

"Why me?" woofed Shep. He didn't want to go anywhere *near* that wind.

"No one else can get the door open, silly fur." Callie headed for the door to Higgins's den — they'd left it open, so as not to get trapped.

"My teeth hurt from biting *that* knob," said Shep. "I'm not going to risk breaking a fang." He ran his paw over his muzzle for emphasis. Who was Callie to tell him to follow her? He was the big dog, the rescuer — he'd saved her from a giant killer bird! Why was he the one getting pushed around?

"That dog sounds like it's in trouble. I'm going!" Callie raced out of the den. Frizzle took off after her, howling with delight.

"Finally," sighed Higgins. "Some peace and quiet!" He snuggled back down in the comforter.

Shep looked at the bed, and at Higgins, already snoring away. *Why, Great Wolf, did I ever leave my den?*

Shep bolted out of the door, sniffing his way after Callie. She was only going to get herself into trouble, and it wasn't likely that Frizzle would be much help getting her out of it.

He found them both outside a door not far down the hall from Higgins's den. Callie, being a stubborn little mutt, was leaping at the knob, trying to snap her teeth around it.

"Great Wolf," Shep barked, pushing Frizzle aside. "You're never going to get the knob to turn that way."

Shep heard scratching on the other side of the door. "Well, dock my tail! Is that Shep?"

Shep knew that voice: It was Zeus! Shep barked hello, his tail spastic with joy at running into his best friend.

"Zeus! Thank the Great Wolf!" Shep yipped, leaping at the door. "What's the trouble?"

Zeus explained that a tree outside his den had crashed through the window. "Rain's pouring in," he barked, "and the wall's broken."

"Don't worry," woofed Shep. "I'm going to get you out."

Shep attacked the knob with all his strength. He dug his teeth into its hard skin and scrabbled his paws against the door frame. He twisted his head up and down, side to side. Still, the door did not open.

"There must be something wrong with this knob," growled Shep. He leapt down from the door, panting. "Go get Higgins," he barked to Frizzle.

"You're not the alpha of me," Frizzle snorted back.

"For the love of treats!" Callie snapped at both of their snouts. "Just go get him!" she yowled.

Frizzle snorted and trotted down the hall. "I'm going," he grumbled, "but only because *she* asked."

Zeus dug at the floor with his paws.

"Just wait a heartbeat," barked Shep. "There's this little yapper in the den down the hall who knows about human stuff."

"What are you doing with all these yappers, anyway?" said Zeus, lying down and pressing his snout against the space at the bottom of the door.

"These *yappers* are the ones who are trying to save you," growled Callie.

"Sorry," grumbled Zeus, not sounding at all sorry. "But really, Shep. What are you doing here?"

Shep explained about his den, how his boy had left him, and the lack of water. "Then this little — er, Callie helped me to escape. While we were exploring the streets, she got attacked by this huge bird, and I saved her."

"Wow!" barked Zeus. "Bird fight! Awesome!"

"If you're done with the big dog talk," growled Callie, "can we get back to the rescue?"

Higgins stumbled toward them, with Frizzle nipping at his rump.

"All right! All right!" Higgins yapped. "I'm awake!" He yawned, then squinted at the door. "What's the problem? Won't open?"

Shep wagged his tail in affirmation.

Higgins snorted. "Dog on the other side of the door?"

"It's Zeus, you little furface."

Callie looked at Higgins. "You know each other?" she asked.

"Unfortunately," growled Zeus from the space under the door.

"Ah, pleasant as always. Just like a boxer. Well, Zeus, is there a little nub on the knob on your side of the door?"

They heard Zeus scramble to his paws. "I think so. There's a bump, like a little knob inside the big knob."

"It's as I thought," said Higgins. "The door's locked."

"So what do I do?" barked Shep, ears pricked, tail up

and waving. He was losing patience. Why was there always so much barking before the doing? He had to save his friend!

"Nothing," yipped Higgins. "A locked door is a locked door. I don't think that big fuzz head Zeus could figure out how to turn the lock."

"When I get out of here, you're going to pay for that fuzz head remark," growled Zeus.

"If you get out of there, I'll worry," yapped Higgins.

"Enough!" howled Callie. "My fur, you boydogs are silly. This isn't some marking contest. What if that terrible wind comes back? We have to save Zeus, and quick. So, Higgins, tell us how to turn the lock, and, Zeus, stop grumbling like an empty belly!"

All the dogs stared at the little girldog. Callie stood tall, chest out, tail high and still, teeth bared and jowls trembling.

Higgins cleared his throat. "Yes. Well. All right." He cowered a bit as he passed Callie, then barked instructions to Zeus through the door on how to turn the little nub on the knob. "I managed to get on a table and turn the one on our knob, so it shouldn't be *too* difficult for you, I'd wager."

Shep heard the low rumble of Zeus's growl and wondered if it wouldn't be best for Higgins to head back to his den. There was some scratching at the door, some more growling, then a click.

"I think I did it," Zeus yipped.

Shep attacked the door with everything he had left in him. After a few heartbeats' struggle, the door swung open. This time, Shep had the sense to let go of the knob before the door pulled him into the den. He got knocked to the floor anyway when Zeus jumped on top of him.

"You're the best!" Zeus howled, leaping to his paws, his stumpy tail waggling. Zeus looked as if he'd just landed in a pile of jerky, he was so happy.

"Yeah, well, get off me before you break something," Shep said, grinning.

A voice squeaked from beneath Shep's shoulder. "You already did!"

Shep quickly rolled over, and off of poor little Higgins! Shep had squashed him when Zeus pounced.

"This is what I meant when I called you a fuzz head, you fuzz heads!" Higgins shook himself all over and began scratching his ears. "Now I have lint in my ears and probably a broken rib! Big dogs never think, never look around to see if they're about to sit on a dog's snout."

Zeus snorted and sat back on his haunches. "It's not the big dog's job to watch out who's under his butt. It's the little dog's job to keep out of the way."

"It's the little dog who just *saved* that big dog's butt," Callie snapped. "So the big dog had better look before he sits, got it?" She stuck her muzzle right in Zeus's snout, her chest puffed out and hackles raised.

Zeus began to growl and raise his hackles.

*This is not going to end well*, thought Shep. He stuck his nose in. "How about we promise to look before we sit, and you watch for falling butts. Okay? Every dog happy?" He opened his jowls, panting in a friendly manner, and wagged his tail.

Callie and Zeus stared at each other for a few heartbeats more, then Callie stepped back.

"Listen," she woofed, her head cocked.

"That's my Callie!" yipped Frizzle, cuffing Higgins on the ear with his paw. "Is she a fierce little thing or what?"

Shep heard something: a wail. Not wind, definitely dog.

"I'm going back to bed," Higgins grumbled.

"We can't go back to bed," Callie barked. "Didn't you hear that howl? We have to check all the dens."

"No," said Zeus. "We don't. Those other dogs can take care of themselves."

"How would you have liked it if we'd said that about you?" growled Callie. She flicked her snout at Zeus's den's open door. Through it, Shep saw the broken window and the palm fronds flapping through it. Fat raindrops spattered the floor inside, blown in on a gust of wind that ruffled the fur on Shep's muzzle. The wall around the window was cracked. Splintered beams jutted through the gap and the bottom half of the wall sagged into the den. The storm's claws scratched at the very walls of the building.

Callie continued, "This is a bad storm, and there are no humans around to help us out. We have to help ourselves." Her tail stood tall, its slight curl trembling.

"Ha-roo!" howled Frizzle. "Let's get this thing going! Big dog," he barked at Zeus, "how about you and me start on the next door?"

Zeus looked ready to trounce the squat yapper. In an effort to keep the fur on every dog's back, Shep got off his haunches and strode to Callie's side.

"Callie," he woofed, "it's not that Zeus and I don't want to help." He shot a quick glance at Zeus, hoping he'd play along. "But freeing the dogs isn't as easy as all that. All you have to do is stand there, while Zeus and I do all the hard work of opening the knobs. I nearly broke a tooth getting that one open." He swung his snout toward Zeus's door. "And we don't even know where that dog is — it could be Outside, in the storm!"

Callie's tail drooped. "So you won't help us?" she whimpered. "But what about that other dog? What if she was hurt by that awful wind? What if she's trapped and scared, like I was out on that grate? I can't bear to think of another dog suffering like that when there's something that I can do to help." She began to tremble again. She sat and scratched limply at her ear.

Frizzle set his little jaw and paraded across the hall to Callie's side, looking at Shep like he'd attacked the miserable girldog, like it was all his fault.

"Don't you worry, gorgeous," Frizzle woofed. "You and me, we'll find that dog and free any others we scent along the way." He licked her jowl, and Callie smiled at him and waggled her tail.

"Oh, Great Wolf." Shep sighed. "We'll search this floor, okay?" He glanced at Zeus, who narrowed his eyes and snorted loudly.

Callie was instantly on her paws, tail wagging, nose sniffing the air. "Brilliant! Shep, you come with me, and Zeus, you go with Higgins and Frizzle."

Zeus didn't even address Callie. He turned to Shep and began grumbling. "We're taking orders from the yappers now?" He spat the words out like slobber.

"There's bound to be other big dogs in this building," Shep said, trying to soothe his friend. "They can help out with freeing the other dogs."

"I've lived here for three cycles," Zeus growled. "There are maybe three or four other big dogs, and I know at least one of them has got one paw in the hole, if you know what I mean." Zeus referred to any dog who was in less than top condition as having "one paw in the hole," so Shep wasn't sure whether he meant the dog was old or simply had gone a little overboard with the kibble.

"It's one floor, buddy," Shep said, panting gently. "Then we can all get some sleep."

"Fine," Zeus barked. "But I'm not going with those two mutts." He trotted over to Callie's side. "You're so anxious to get started?" he grunted at her. "Let's move." Zeus continued down the hall and around the corner.

Callie looked at Frizzle, eyebrows raised as if to say it was better than nothing, and raced after the big dog.

"I'm going back to my den," yapped Higgins. "Hang all these other ungrateful mutts." With a quick flick of his grizzled snout, he was up and on his way down the hall to his den.

"Looks like it's just you and me." Frizzle opened his jaws and panted in self-satisfied huffs, his wing-ears tipped to the sides in what Shep understood to be as close to content as they ever got. Frizzle swaggered down the hall in the direction opposite the way Callie had gone, then looked back over his tail at Shep. "You coming?"

Shep growled to himself, *Great Wolf, give me strength.*

# CHAPTER 7
## FRIZZLE

"Callie tells me you're a fighter?" Frizzle sniffed lazily at a door, then loped down the stone floor of the hall to the next one.

"Was," Shep barked, checking the door Frizzle had just sniffed. "*Was* a fighter." He snorted, then took a deep breath, fully scenting the air. It was as he thought — that yapper's pug nose was good for nothing. "There's a dog in here."

"What?!" Frizzle scrambled back, nearly head-butting Shep. "Let me smell it again." He stuck his nose practically under the door and began snorting and snuffling. "Oh, yeah. There is a *faint* smell of dog." He straightened his forelegs and licked his nose. "Very faint.

Any dog could've missed that scent." He scratched his neck, shook his coat, then tipped his head at Shep. "Well?"

"Well, what?" Shep woofed. Wasn't Frizzle going to apologize, or something? He nearly left a dog behind because he was too lazy to take a proper scent!

"You going to open the door or wait and see if it opens itself?" Frizzle jutted out his wide jaw. Shep had the urge to swipe it right off his tiny smug snout.

Shep grumbled to himself. *No dog should have to put up with this*, he thought. *Being pushed around by yappers, breaking teeth on stupid knobs.* He attacked the knob, biting and thrashing his head and scrabbling his paws against the door frame. Nothing.

"There must be a lock," Frizzle said, yawning. "You should check with the dog inside."

*I'll check you, you little . . .* Shep hopped down onto all fours, and barked loudly at the door. "Hey! Dog! You smell like a big dog, am I right?"

He heard claws clicking on the floor. Taking a deep sniff, he could tell that it was a girldog, that she was a bit older than Shep, and was about the same size. A tough dog, but not a fighter. *Thank the Great Wolf.* Shep thought he might've chewed his own ears off if he'd had to take care of another yapper.

"Hello?" barked the girldog. "Yes, I'm a chocolate Labrador retriever."

"What is *that*?" yapped Frizzle.

"You must be a mutt," she moaned. "It's so hard to find a purebred dog these suns."

"Who you calling a mutt, you choco-triever, or whatever you are?" Frizzle's hackles were up. He looked ready to fight the door frame.

Shep sighed and sat on his haunches. This was worse than a yapper — he had a snob on his hands. Shep knew these dogs from the Park. Dogs with fancy collars who thought the world of themselves, looking down their muzzles at the rest of the pack.

"Purebred or not, we're here to rescue you," Shep barked.

"Thank you, but I'm perfectly fine as is."

Shep heard the clicking of the girldog's paws, then nothing. She must have gone back to bed. She had the right idea.

"What are we doing?" Shep growled. "Let's just tell Callie we checked the rest of the hallway and get back to bed."

"You can go back to the den," said Frizzle. "I'm checking the rest of the hall." He picked up his nub of a tail and trotted away from Shep, nose in the air.

Shep whined and stared longingly down the hall at the open doorway of Higgins's den, the nice dark place where he could wait out this storm in peace, all curled up on that giant bed, thinking only of the return to his own den, and his own boy, and his own yapper-free life. Then he got up and followed that stumpy, black, pug-nosed, little demon-dog Frizzle.

"So, you were telling me about your fighting suns," Frizzle said as Shep caught up with him.

Shep didn't recall saying anything of the kind. "No, I wasn't," he woofed. "I don't like to bark about it."

Frizzle sniffed a door, properly this time, taking a number of snorty breaths. "Aw, come on. All dogs like to bark about their fights. This one time, at the Park near my den, I got into it with this dog who was almost a full-stretch taller than me. He thought I'd be easy pickings, but he learned a thing or two." Frizzle panted loudly, grinning. "Dog, you should have seen his nose when I got through with him. I was all, CLAW, CLAW, right in his snout." Frizzle danced back and forth on his hind legs, swiping his paws in the air.

Shep stepped back to avoid the flailing little yapper. It was almost too funny to watch him scrabble around. As if that was how you fought another dog. Frizzle looked like he was trying to catch a Ball with his paws, like a human!

"I'm sure it was a thrilling battle," Shep woofed sarcastically.

Frizzle quit his air-dance and snorted loudly. "Yeah, well. I've shown the dogs in that Park a thing or two."

"I'm sure you have." Shep could barely keep from bursting into a fit of panting. This dog was ridiculous!

"Nothing in this den but a cat," Frizzle yipped. "You agree, Mister Big Nose?" He cocked his head at Shep.

"Call me that again," Shep growled.

"What?" Frizzle snorted. "You going to do something about it?" Frizzle's tail waggled and his jaws split into a snaggle-toothed smile. He hopped on his little paws. "Come on, Big Nose. One fight. I'll show you all my best moves." He slapped his paws on the ground. A thread of drool dangled from his bottom lip.

Shep sighed. Much as he wanted to bury Frizzle in a pile of sand, he wasn't a dog who trounced yappers for the fun of it. Fighting — real fighting — wasn't a game to be played, especially with such an easy mark. "Maybe some other time," he woofed.

"Really?" Frizzle yipped. "Because I've wanted to try this new move. I call it the cockroach. See, I get real low, then scuttle under the other dog's belly. . . ."

This parade of crazy continued for the next several doors. Frizzle would try to get Shep to bark about his fighting suns, and when he refused, Frizzle would act out another of his infamous battles. With each display, Shep became more and more certain that the little dog had never fought so much as a dead squirrel. But he let him go on, and the battles Frizzle described became more and more fantastical.

"This one time, I had three — no, four — dogs on me at once. I was kicking with my hind legs — BAM, CLAW — and slashing with my jaws — FANG, FANG, FANG — and my fore claws, whew! They were invisible, moving fast as the wind — PAW, PAW, PAW."

He had an active imagination. Shep had to give Frizzle that.

"I think we've got one," Shep barked loudly, interrupting the severe thrashing Frizzle was giving to his shadow.

"All right!" Frizzle howled, panting heavily from his exertions. "Smells like a little dog. Fluffy one. One of those little white fluffy things, I'm guessing."

Frizzle was getting better at scenting things out. Shep agreed that they were looking at freeing the worst kind of yapper — the tiny, breakable kind.

"Hey, fluffy dog!" Frizzle yapped. "You need rescuing?" He pounced on the door, scratching at the metal.

Tiny claws ticked on the floor stones, and there was the whisper of fur dragging on the ground. "Please! It's dark in here," the fluffy dog woofed. "I'm lonely, and the wind is making such an awful racket." The girldog's voice was raspy, and she smelled like an old timer.

The fact that she was an old timer changed everything for Shep. He crouched low, close to the door, and woofed softly to her. "I need you to look up at the knob on the door. Is there a little nub on it?" The girldog said yes, and Shep explained to her about locks and how she needed to turn that nub.

"Is there a table near the door?" Frizzle barked. "Can you get on it and turn the nub?"

The old timer whimpered. "No, there's no table. Does that mean you can't get me out?" She lay down and pressed her nose to the space at the bottom of the door. "The light's so dim in the hall. I wish it were brighter. It's so dark in here."

Shep put his head down to the floor and snuffled at the old girldog. "I'm sorry," he whined. "I wish we could dig through this door and get you out."

"It's all right." She sighed. "My mistress will be back soon."

Shep didn't have the heart to tell her about the empty streets, how everything seemed abandoned, about the iguanas parading down the Sidewalk, how he hadn't seen a human in suns. He didn't want to think about these things himself. How could he tell a poor, trapped old timer that her mistress might never return?

"She will," Shep said. "Just curl up and I'm sure she'll be back in the morning."

Shep waited until he could no longer hear the click and shuffle of the old timer's stride. By the time he turned around, Frizzle was already halfway down the hall, headed back to Higgins's den. They'd finished the entire hallway, and didn't have a single rescue to show for it. Shep trotted to catch up with Frizzle.

"Sad to have to leave her behind," Frizzle yapped when Shep reached his side. "But that's the nature of things, right? The Law of the Land — only the strong survive." Frizzle added an extra swish to his waddle as he spoke.

*Nature didn't trap that old timer*, Shep brooded. But he kept quiet, not wanting to let Frizzle see how much leaving behind the girldog had rattled him.

Frizzle glanced up at Shep and stopped. "Why's your tail dragging?"

*Stupid tail!* Shep growled at his rump like it had a traitorous mind of its own.

"It's not that old timer, is it?" Frizzle's tail wagged, like he knew he was onto something.

Shep braced himself for an attack. Frizzle sensed his weakness; Shep knew that any weakness was an opening.

But Frizzle didn't attack. He dropped his head, lowered his ears (as far as he could), and wagged his tail.

"Don't worry about her," Frizzle said. "She was just a little scared. And she was an old dog. I give her one, two cycles, tops. Her best suns are long gone." Frizzle panted happily, as if these points made everything all right.

These little dogs confused Shep. Here was a clear opening for a fight and Frizzle didn't take it. Instead, he tried to be friendly. In an awful kind of way, he was trying to comfort Shep. Frizzle didn't know about the old timer in the fight kennel; he was just a cocky pup who was trying to be nice. Well, Shep didn't need his niceness. He was the big dog. He was a rescuer. He didn't need to be comforted by a know-nothing, yappy braggart like Frizzle.

"Just because she's old doesn't mean she's worthless," Shep grumbled. "And if the law is only the strong survive, how do *you* expect to make it?"

Frizzle snorted. "Touchy, touchy, Mister Big Nose. Come on. We have to meet up with Callie." He waddled toward the entry.

Shep watched the little dog until he turned the corner, then followed. Things were less confusing for Shep when he was alone. Then there were only his needs, only his fears.

He looked inside Zeus's den. The crack in the wall was black with wet, and a new crack had scratched its way across the ceiling. A puddle stretched from below the broken window to the open doorway. Small tongues of water licked at the stones of the hall.

Shep pressed his body to the opposite wall as he passed, as if dipping his paws in the puddle would infect him with the storm's destruction. The den's ceiling groaned like it was in pain. A dog howled somewhere above. There were others trapped in this building. Other dogs desperate for Shep to help them.

*I can barely help myself,* Shep thought. He looked out the window at the end of the hall — still dark. Thick sheets of rain glittered in the darkness, warping the light from the buildings across the way. The storm's smell was everywhere, and when the wind gusted, the pounding of the rain against the glass was deafeningly loud. He'd never smelled anything like this storm. Was there any chance it would be over by morning? How long until he could leave all these yappers behind and go back to his den and forget their problems and needs and fears?

Callie and Zeus were waiting in the entry room. Callie sniffed the potted palms that stood on either side of the entry doors, while Zeus was collapsed in a pile against the opposite wall. Trembling in the hallway beyond stood a yellowish, medium-sized girldog with a long fat tail, floppy ears, and tapered snout ending in a brown nose. She stared miserably at the single step that led from the hall into the entry room.

Frizzle scrambled over to Callie and gave her a couple of licks on the nose. "What's up with the yellow dog?" he snuffled, tilting his head in the girldog's general direction.

"I think she's afraid of steps," Callie said. "She's a little nervous about doors and steps. Her name's Boji, short for Beaujolais."

"Nice to meet you, Bo-jellies!" Frizzle barked, tail wagging.

The yellow dog glanced at him, gave a feeble wave of her tail, then looked back at the step like it might take a snap at her.

Shep loped over to where Zeus lay, spread out between the blue wall and the counter. Zeus looked at Shep like he was ready to gnaw his own tail off.

"I don't know how you put up with it," Zeus whined. "The incessant yapping: 'Try it this way,' 'Let's get that door.' I'm about ready to lock myself back in my den and take my chances with the storm."

"I hear you, buddy," Shep moaned, flopping down beside him.

Zeus wagged his tail. "The yellow dog is a little off," he said. "We found one other dog, but his door had some sort of chain holding it shut. We called the Furface over to help, but he had no idea what to do." Zeus had apparently taken to calling Higgins "the Furface."

"We had one snob who wanted to be left in her den," Shep woofed. "And one old timer girldog who couldn't undo the lock on her door." Shep licked his paws, hoping to hide from Zeus how upset he was about the old timer.

"Good riddance," Zeus said. "Last thing we need is a pain in the tail purebred and an old yapper."

"Yeah," Shep replied, trying to sound casual. He tried to push from his mind the image of the old timer alone and scared in the dark. Why couldn't he be like Zeus? He didn't want to care about these other dogs! But still, the feelings pressed on him like heavy paws. Shep even felt bad about leaving the snobby purebred behind. What if a tree broke her window? She might wish she'd taken Shep up on his rescue offer, but it'd be too late.

"I smell twelve other dogs," Callie barked loudly from within a tangle of leaves. "Frizzle says you only found two, which means there are still ten dogs trapped in this building."

"I heard a howl from above Zeus's den," Shep woofed.

Callie burst out of the plant and slid to the middle of the entry room. "Then we've got to get up there," she yapped.

Zeus stood and shook himself. "I don't care if there are fifty dogs still trapped in this building, I'm going to bed."

"I wouldn't go back to your den, dog," Frizzle woofed. "Not unless you're looking to take a Bath."

"I'll go where I want, yapper," Zeus growled.

"Fine," Frizzle snarled. "You smell like you could use a Bath, anyway."

Zeus whirled like a wind and snapped his teeth a whisker-length from Frizzle's snout. The little dog was so startled, he peed.

Zeus panted as he lifted his head. "Not so tough now, eh?" He loped into the dark of Higgins's den.

Callie crept toward Frizzle, tail low. "You okay?" she snuffled.

Frizzle shook himself. "Why wouldn't I be?" he grunted. "Big fuzz head. Had to sneak up on me, see that? He knew I'd get him in a fair fight." He licked Callie on the nose.

She raised her wagging tail. "Yeah," she yipped. "I know you would."

Callie turned to Shep. "We'd best get moving on finding those other dogs. You'll help me, right?"

Shep lifted his head. Callie's eyes were wide and hopeful, and her little tail wagged back and forth. She panted lightly, mouth open, jowls curled up, and her ears bobbed with each breath. How could Shep say no to that muzzle?

"Yeah, Big Nose," yapped Frizzle. "You'll help us."

There it was — the reason to say no. But then he thought of the cracked wall and the howl from above, of that scared old-timer, of how frightened he'd been without food and water. How could he sleep when he knew other dogs were in trouble, feeling desperate and alone? It wouldn't take too long to check the other floors. And soon it would be light out and the storm would be over and he could go home. Why not help them out this one last time?

"Fine," Shep barked. "But how do we get up to these other floors? There's a stairwell in my building, but I don't see a stairwell here."

The yellow dog began panting and wagging her tail excitedly. "I know!" she barked. "Those metal doors over there." She waved her nose at the two shiny doors in the wall behind Shep. "They open, and then the box behind the doors goes up."

"Brilliant!" yipped Callie. "Can you open them?"

"I would," whimpered Boji. "But there's this step." She looked down at the step, as if perhaps the other dogs had not noticed its nefarious presence in the room.

"It's just a step," yapped Frizzle. "Just, you know, step on it."

Boji's eyes opened wide, like Frizzle had just suggested she jump in front of a Car. "Oh, dear," she whined.

"Just take a big jump," yipped Callie. "You'll fly right over that step."

"Really?" asked Boji, her tail wagging.

Callie stood tall and wagged her tail back. "You can do it!"

Boji closed her eyes and leapt off the top of the step, landing in the middle of the entry room. "Did I make it?" she barked loudly, eyes still shut.

"You made it," Frizzle yapped. He leaned slightly away from the trembling Beaujolais.

Boji opened her eyes. "I did it!" she howled. She did a circular happy dance, tail flopping from side to side. "Bless my treats, that was exhilarating!" She shook herself. "Normally, my mistress helps me with those terrible things. Why do they put those cliffs in the floor? Awful! Ridiculous! Humans can be so silly."

Shep was a bit wary of this girldog. He approached with ears forward and eyes and nose open. He sniffed her over, and let her sniff him back. She seemed like a different dog now that she was off the step — very friendly, full of excitement. Her eyes were a soft brown and she smelled good-natured, even toward the little dogs. She was eager to lick Frizzle's snout, and quickly rolled over to show Callie she meant no threat.

"About this metal doorway?" Shep asked, once all four had finished their introductions.

"Oh, yes!" Boji barked. "We just need to push that button." She leapt onto the wall and slapped at a small, lighted circle. Sure enough, the metal doors slid open, revealing a room barely bigger than Shep's crate.

Shep, Callie, and Frizzle trotted into the close room behind the doors, but Boji stayed in the entry hall. She looked down with that same miserable gaze at the metal-lined space in the floor between the entry hall and the small room.

"Aren't you coming?" Callie asked in her friendliest, most encouraging bark.

"Oh, dear," Boji whimpered. She pawed dubiously at the metal in the floor.

And then the doors slipped shut.

Frizzle looked first at Shep, then Callie. "Now what?"

# CHAPTER 8
## LIGHTS OUT

Shep's heart began to race. He did not like this small room; he did not like the metal doors that closed of their own volition. Every few heartbeats, winds roared around the little box, like the storm was licking the very walls. Callie trembled violently and crouched low to the floor. Frizzle began to bark hysterically, which made everything that much worse.

"Hey! Dog! Bo-jellies! Let us out!" Frizzle yelped.

They could hear Boji whimpering on the other side of the door. "Oh, dear. Oh, dear."

Shep scanned the walls of the room. Next to the metal doors were a bunch of small buttons like the one Boji had pushed to open the doors. Maybe one of them would open the doors back up? Shep figured it was better than standing there, heart racing, yapper yapping.

Shep reared and slammed his paws against the buttons. A number of them lit up, and the small room jolted to life. Shep fell back on all fours; his stomach felt like it was sinking into the floor.

"What's happening?" he cried, cringing against the wall.

"I don't know!" squealed Callie. "Make it stop!"

"I know what this is," barked Frizzle. "We have one in my building. It's El Vator."

"El what?!" Shep whimpered.

"El *Vator*," Frizzle yapped calmly. "It's a room that moves from one place to another place."

"It feels like we're going up," Callie said. She stopped trembling and began sniffing at the metal doors. "The air is moving outside El Vator. And I smell different things with each one of those bings."

Shep was trying to keep his kibble in his stomach. These yappers seemed much more at home with this human stuff than he.

And then the lights went out. El Vator shuddered to a halt.

Shep dug his claws into the floor. He was too afraid to breathe.

Two heartbeats. Howling wind.

The lights returned. El Vator rumbled to life and shot upward again, leaving Shep's stomach on the floor below.

"What was that?" he yowled.

"That's never happened to me before in El Vator," Frizzle moaned.

El Vator slowed, and with a final bing, stopped completely. The metal doors slid open. Frizzle and Callie raced out, but it took Shep a heartbeat to catch his breath. Just as he was about to follow them, the doors began to slide closed. Shep leapt off his hind legs and bounded out of El Vator. The doors slipped shut, catching a few hairs off his tail.

Shep stared at the closed metal doors, sucking air like a thing half-drowned. "We are finding *another* way back down," he growled. "I am not stepping paw in El Vator again."

Frizzle and Callie flicked their tails in agreement.

They stood in a hall similar to the ones on the entry floor, only this one didn't have an entry room with clear sliding doors opening onto the street. This made sense, assuming Callie was right and El Vator had taken them up.

"Which way first?" Frizzle asked, sniffing the air down one of the halls. "It smells musty."

"Let's split up," Shep barked. "Frizzle, you sniff that way. Callie, you and I can cover this hall." He wasn't about to get stuck hearing about Frizzle's imaginary fights for another length of hallway.

Frizzle set his little jaw, like he was about to protest, but then he turned and began snuffling along a door frame. Shep heard him grumble to himself under his snorty breaths.

"I'll take this door," said Callie, trotting up to the nearest one. "You start on the next." She sounded disappointed and kept glancing over her tail at where Frizzle had gone.

Shep walked to where Callie was sniffing. He didn't want to bully her into dropping that Frizzle like a spitting cat, but he hoped to point her to the right scent (not Frizzle's), like the old timer had done for him back in the fight kennel.

"That Frizzle seems to like you quite a bit." He kept his bark as calm as possible.

Callie's ears pricked forward. "You think so?" She grinned. "He smells like a sun-warmed bed, doesn't he?" Callie bent her nose back to the door and took several deep sniffs. "This one smells empty — wait, there's a rodent of some kind. Or maybe a cat who just ate a rodent? Nope — rodent, I'm sure. We've really clicked, you know?"

"Who? You and the rodent?" He hated when his conversations with Callie got all twisty.

"No, silly fur, Frizzle." Callie trotted to the next door and Shep followed.

"But how can you stand that little yap — dog?" Shep grumbled. He sniffed the gap below the door: no dogs.

"He's very, I don't know, up?" Callie replied, flicking her tail at the thought. "He's so excited about everything. It's how I felt getting to run on the streets this morning. Like the whole world was full of good things for me."

Shep had to agree that Frizzle was definitely an "up" kind of dog. Only Shep found Frizzle's incessant yammering and ridiculous fantasies of everything as going his way annoying.

"Are you sure he isn't" — Shep dug for the right word — "crazy? All he barks about is fighting and I'm pretty sure he's never so much as sniffed another dog's rump."

Callie cocked her head. "Are you *jealous*?"

Shep instantly started to backtrack. "Jealous? Of what? You and Frizzle? No. I mean, you're a yapper. I'm a big dog. The rescuer."

"Then why are you growling about Frizzle and me getting along?" Callie sniffed a door. "Ferret."

"I just think there are other kibbles in the dish, you know?" Shep woofed. "Better kibbles. Ones that don't yap constantly about fighting."

Callie snapped at Shep's ruff. "Worry less about my kibbles and more about what's in your own dish." She trotted to the next door.

Maybe Shep was a little jealous of Frizzle. Not about Callie, but about his being so "up." Crazy as Frizzle was, he seemed happy. Shep had to admit, it would be nice to feel like the world was full of good things for him. Right now, the only thing he felt was like everything in his world either hurt his teeth or yapped at him.

"I think I found one!" Callie yipped.

Shep joined her and scented the den: a big dog, older. The dog smelled nervous.

"Dog!" Shep barked. He heard shuffling claws on the floor — long hair, a mid-weight dog, lighter than Shep.

"Hi!" said the big dog. "My name's Wensleydale."

"What kind of name is *that*?" yipped Callie.

"It's a cheese," answered the dog. "I'm an English setter and it's an English cheese."

"Well, Wednesday-dale, Wellesley —" Shep began. *Couldn't something be easy?* he grumbled. *Bad! Think positive!*

"You can just call me Cheese, if you'd like," woofed the dog.

"Well, Cheese," Shep said, feeling like maybe this thinking positive had some fur on it, "I need you to look at the door. There's a paw on it called a knob."

"Oh, yes," Cheese said. "I know about these things. It's just that this door is so heavy. I can't get it open."

*Thank the Great Wolf, my teeth are saved!* Thinking positive was working already! "If you turn the knob," Shep barked, "I can push the door in."

"Brilliant!" yipped Callie, her tail in full swing.

It took a few tries, but Shep and Cheese finally got the door open. Cheese bounded into the hallway. He was as tall as Shep, but skinny, and covered in silky, longish white fur dappled with dark gray spots. His long snout had rather droopy jowls, and his ears dangled far below his jaw and were covered in the same silky fur.

Once they were properly introduced, Shep sent Cheese off to find Frizzle and help him rescue any dogs on his part of the hallway. Though Cheese was too light to pull open the metal doors, he was plenty strong enough to push them open. Shep and Callie continued sniffing doors along their hall, but came up with nothing.

"Let's head back toward El Vator," Callie barked.

Just as she took her first step, the lights went out.

"Callie!" Shep barked.

One heartbeat.

Lights came on, but not the dim ceiling lights. In their place shone two blindingly bright spotlights. They glowed from a point high on the wall not far from where Shep stood.

Callie trembled a stretch away from Shep. "What's happening?" she whined. "Where'd the lights go?"

"Shep! Callie!" It was Frizzle. He came bounding out of the dark and ran directly to Callie. The instant he saw her, his stubby tail waggled and he started panting with joy. "Thank my Master, you're all right!" He licked her jowls, and she panted and growled and pawed playfully at his fat head.

Cheese loped into view, followed by two yappers — a fawn-colored, chubby, smush-nosed girldog with triangular black flap-ears and a long, skinny brown pup with stumpy legs and floppy ears that nearly dragged on the floor.

"The pug's Daisy, and the little dachshund's Oscar," Cheese woofed, tail wagging in its friendly way.

"Where'd the lights — *snort* — go?" Daisy asked.

Her tightly-wound tail wagged as best it could. Oscar, who was two, maybe three moons old, stayed pressed to Daisy's side, eyes wide and tail between his legs.

"We tried to open El Vator," Frizzle yapped. "But the button doesn't work."

"There has to be another way down," barked Callie.

"What if there isn't?" grumbled Shep. It was hard to stay positive in the dark with a bunch of strange dogs and no boy.

"There is," woofed Cheese. He looked cheerfully at Shep, then Callie, tail flopping side to side.

"And?" asked Frizzle. "You want to share with the rest of us?"

"Oh, sure," he barked, then loped into the dark.

"Wait for us!" Callie yipped, running after him.

Frizzle and Daisy raced after Callie, but little Oscar wasn't as fast. He tripped over his own paws.

"You okay?" asked Shep, crouching low so that he was on the little dog's level.

"I miss my mom," Oscar whimpered. He didn't even look at Shep; he stared at the floor.

Shep licked Oscar's head, nearly knocking him over. Oscar grinned, panting short, sweet breaths, then remembered he was miserable and went back to staring at the floor.

"Shep! We found a door!" Callie's voice echoed from down the hall. Shep smelled that the other dogs were already out of the hallway.

"Come on, Oscar," Shep woofed softly. "We'll get you out of this dark hall and then try to find your mom."

"Really?" he asked, eyes wide and tail wagging. "Okay."

Shep walked slowly beside Oscar, letting him set the pace. Oscar didn't say anything, but he glanced at Shep's paws every few steps, as if making sure he was still beside him.

Callie was waiting for them in an open doorway at the end of the hall with Cheese, who sat with his rump against the door, holding it open.

"What took you so lon — oh." Callie knelt down and gave Oscar a sniff. "Can you walk down stairs?" she asked him.

Oscar looked past her. Beyond the doorway was a stairwell that echoed with the barks of the other dogs mixed with the shrieks of the storm winds. At the end of each run of steps, there was a landing, above which was one of the blinding spotlights that had come on when the regular lights went out.

"I've never been down steps," Oscar whimpered.

Callie trotted to the landing's edge. "It's like this," she yipped, hopping down onto the first step. "See?" She hopped back up. She repeated her hop, first down the step, then back up.

Oscar began to tremble. "Where's Daisy? I want to go home!" he whined.

Callie stood on the step with her bottom front fang caught on her jowl, giving her the strangest expression. She stared at the step as if it might give her the answer. Cheese smiled blankly at Shep, tail wiggling, clearly unable to help solve the problem at paw.

"I'll carry him," Shep said. "I saw a mother carry a pup once at the kennel. If I can get a good enough hold on him, I think I can get him down the steps."

Callie sprang up the step and leapt at Shep's snout, licking and nipping at his jowls. "You wonderful big old furball!"

Shep was doing it: He was thinking positive. He was being "up." *Bring on the good things!*

Little Oscar trembled near Shep's front paws.

"I've got you," Shep woofed. He snuffled his muzzle along Oscar's back until he felt enough give in the pup's thin fur. He took up the skin in his teeth and bit down. The pup yelped; Shep let go and the little dog plopped back onto the floor.

"Let's try again," Shep grumbled. It was hard being "up" when everything was difficult.

He bit Oscar's scruff again, trying to close his teeth as gently as possible on the fur. This time, Oscar merely whimpered as Shep lifted him off the floor.

"Let's go!" Shep growled through his teeth.

Callie led the way down the stairs, with Shep and Cheese following. Frizzle and Daisy waited for them on one of the landings.

"Don't go down any farther," Frizzle yipped. "It stinks like rat and mildew. This door smells like the main hall we started on." Frizzle jumped up on the door, pawing in the direction of a bar of metal, which stretched across the door's center where the knob should have been. The bar smelled like a knob: grease and metal.

"I think this is a special knob," Frizzle yapped. "Shep, will you be a friend?"

Shep growled. Wasn't he carrying a pup in his jaws? Wasn't there another big dog *right next to him*?

Shep placed Oscar gently on the floor. "Sure, *friend*. Let me get that for you."

He reared and slapped the knob with his paws to test it out. It clicked open just by pressing down on it. *Why weren't* all *knobs like this?* Shep wondered. He pushed again on the flat part and shoved with his shoulder, and the door swung open into a hall off the entry room. Boji still mumbled miserably in front of the metal doors of El Vator.

"Thanks, Big Nose!" Frizzle yapped, trotting out of the stairwell, ears forward, tail wagging, chest up.

Shep knew from his stance that Frizzle wasn't trying to bully him, wasn't showing off. He was being friendly, in his pushy, yappy way. But still. Shep was doing all the work. He felt like these little dogs, and even the big dogs like Cheese and Boji, and even Callie, should give him more respect. Shep missed his boy. Things were so much easier with him than with these dogs.

Oscar ran into the entry room. "Daisy!" he yipped. "Shep says he can find my mother!" He frisked about in front of Daisy, tripping over his floppy ears and stumbling on his oversized paws.

"He lied," Daisy yapped. "You — *snort* — came from the store. Even if he wanted to, he couldn't find your mom."

Oscar stopped mid-roll. "What's the store?" he whimpered.

Daisy licked the little pup's nose. "Don't worry," she snuffled. "You've got me, kid. We're okay."

Oscar nuzzled into Daisy's ample flank and curled into a ball. He flashed a pair of huge, sad brown eyes at Shep.

*Great Wolf and soggy kibble,* Shep thought. *You do a nice thing like get a pup off a dark hallway and all you get is grief.* Maybe Zeus had the right idea. Maybe it wasn't about being "up." Maybe it was about taking care of yourself first.

"We should search out the other levels," Callie barked. "Shep, Cheese, you coming?"

*Doesn't this yapper ever stop?* Shep nibbled an itch on his hindquarters. No, he wasn't going to run around, following these yappers who barked orders at him like he wasn't the big dog, like he couldn't trounce every single one of them, roll them in the dirt and —

Shep shivered. He was so angry; why was he so angry?

Callie stood in front of him, brown eyes wide, searching his muzzle for a response. Her ears were forward and her curled tail wiggled. "You okay?" she yipped. She stepped toward him, tail now wagging in wide circles.

"I'm okay," Shep woofed. "Just tired. What's the plan?"

# CHAPTER 9
## SO MANY KNOBS, SO LITTLE TIME

The night stretched out like the flights of stairs before Shep: exhausting and seemingly endless. Worse yet, the wall-lights that had flashed on when everything else went dark grew dimmer with each passing heartbeat.

"Three more floors to go," yipped Callie as she trotted past Shep up the steps.

Callie had split the dogs into teams to make clearing the remaining parts of the building easier. Shep and Cheese followed her from floor to floor. Callie sniffed each door, while Shep and Cheese focused on the knobs that needed opening. Frizzle moved with them; he stayed in front of the door leading from the hall into the stairwell, holding it open with his body.

Boji, Oscar, and Daisy remained on the entry floor. Seeing as Boji couldn't move easily around the building — what with vile stairs and villainous doorways blocking every path — she stayed in the entry room and watched little Oscar. Boji was a natural dam, and she nuzzled and licked Oscar as if he were her own pup. Daisy, like Frizzle, sat holding a door open — this one leading from the stairwell to the entry room.

Cheese bounded up to Shep with a large, brown and black wirehaired dog with a square head and long snout. Long, stiff hairs hung from his jowls near the nose like a hairface. Somehow, on a big dog, it didn't look as ridiculous as it did on Higgins.

"This is Virgil," Cheese said, tail waving. "He's pretty strong — pulled the door open himself."

Virgil tipped his head. "Terrier, Airedale class, at your service."

Shep stood tall and approached Virgil with ears forward and head high. Virgil allowed Shep to sniff him, not submitting to Shep, but not trying to otherwise assert dominance.

"Can I be of assistance?" asked Virgil after Shep stepped back.

"Great Wolf, yes you can!" Shep barked. Those were the best woofs he'd heard all night.

"Two more floors," Callie yipped, trotting past the big dogs.

The whimpers and cries of frightened dogs echoed up the steps and down the halls, filling the building and rivaling the howl of the storm Outside. In the end, they freed Virgil, a lean greyhound named Snoop, an old timer black hunting dog named Dover, and two more yappers: a schnauzer named Rufus, who was the blockiest looking dog Shep had ever seen — square head, rectangular body with bushy-furred legs and a silver hairface — and a snobby sheltie named Ginny, who was covered in poofy brown and white hair and repeatedly mentioned in emphatic moans her distant relationship to some dog named "Lassie."

Virgil loped up the stairwell toward Shep. "Last floor clear?"

"Yup," Shep woofed. "Callie and Frizzle are already headed back to the entry room. There was another chain, but we rescued the rest."

Virgil growled. "I hate to leave a dog behind."

Shep panted lightly — it was nice to hear another dog say what he felt inside. "At least we're done with the hard work, right?" he yipped, a scampish grin on his jowls. He batted Virgil's ear playfully.

Virgil furrowed his brow and cocked his head. "You want to play?" he barked. "At a time like this?"

Apparently, Virgil did not feel *exactly* the same way Shep did. "No," Shep woofed. "Just a bug." He started down the steps. "Never mind."

A thunderous roar echoed around Virgil and Shep. They were near the top end of the staircase, high above the entry floor and as close to the storm as a dog could get.

The monster wind from before growled in Shep's memory — it was back! "We have to get out of here," he barked.

The floor began to vibrate.

Virgil nervously eyed the ceiling. "I agree," he woofed.

They trotted down the steps. At each turn of the staircase, the storm rumbled louder and the building shivered. Two flights down, there was a crack of thunder that rattled the dim lights to darkness. Shep and Virgil raced on in the dark, paws flying down the steps. Another flight down, and they heard a whooshing noise that got louder and louder, so loud it seemed to be sucking at their very whiskers. The floor began to shake hard, forcing them to stop on the next landing. There was a deafening shriek, and the ceiling above them splintered, then exploded up into the sky. The wind tore at Shep's skin, sucking him up.

"I've got you!" barked Virgil. He clamped his jaws around Shep's scruff.

Shep clawed against the pull of the wind. Bits of the building flew up into the clouds, and with them went scraps of each den: couches and tables, and Shep swore he saw a cat disappear into the spinning air.

Then the winds stopped. Shep fell against Virgil. As suddenly as it'd appeared, the voracious wind was gone.

"Thanks," Shep whimpered, climbing off of Virgil. He shook and felt a twinge of pain where Virgil had grabbed him.

"Just doing my duty," woofed Virgil.

Above them, the stairs that remained stood black against a blue sky. The first tails of dawn wagged across wispy clouds high above. It was as if, along with the roof, the storm, too, had disappeared in the screaming wind.

The building groaned, then slumped down on one side. The walls around them cracked and a piece of staircase fell past them down into the dark.

"That's not good," whined Shep. "Let's get out of this stairwell!"

Shep and Virgil raced down what stairs remained and

burst into the entry room. The rescued dogs stood huddled at its center, eyes wide and fur trembling. Callie sniffed around in the potted bushes near the clear entry doors.

The ceiling slanted toward Higgins's den and the door frame to the den was cracked.

"Zeus!" Shep yelped.

Zeus ambled out of the den. "What happened to the ceiling?" he grunted, yawning.

Shep sighed with relief at seeing his friend. Higgins scuttled out of the den behind Zeus, mumbling about how his master would be furious and something about an escaped moth, but perked up when he saw that there were new canine subjects to research.

Zeus's tongue circled his jowls and his stomach gurgled. "Whoa! Hear that? The big dog's hungry. We need to find some kibble!" he barked loudly. He turned to Shep. "Think you can hunt up some kib, the way you've unearthed so many yappers?" Zeus nipped Shep's scruff and panted.

Shep winced — Zeus had bitten him right where Virgil had snagged him back from the wind. "I think we have a little more to worry about than your stomach," Shep grumbled. "For example, the building collapsing on our snouts."

"Problem solved," Zeus barked. He walked up to the clear entry doors. They stayed shut.

"Hey, which one of you yappers broke the door?" he growled.

"Like we didn't try that already," Callie snapped. "The storm broke the doors."

The building grumbled loudly, and with a squeal, the ceiling dropped a whisker-length and the clear doors cracked into huge spiderwebs.

Zeus scampered back, tripping over the pack of terrified dogs.

"If the doors are broken, how can we get out?" Ginny yowled, which started the whole mess of them howling and whimpering. The fear smell was like a fog around Shep. All of the dogs were terrified, even Zeus, who crouched close to the ground and whose ears lay back on his head.

Shep had an idea. "We can get out!" he bellowed. "Cheese, you other big dogs, push over those trees!"

Shep jumped over Higgins and threw all his weight against the potted palm nearest the doors. It rocked, tapping the clear wall of the door, then bounced back into place.

"Hey, Shep!" barked Snoop. "You-want-me-to-push-on-this-tree-huh-yeah-'cause-I-could-push-on-it-yup-yup-see?" He slammed his long, thin legs against a flowering bush.

"No, Snoop!" Shep cried.

But Snoop's single slap was enough to topple the bush; it landed on Ginny with a muffled crunch.

Ginny scrambled out from beneath the bush, leaves and sticks and petals jutting out every which way from her fur. "Lassie never had to suffer such indignities," she grumbled.

"Nice pawwork, Skinny," yapped Frizzle.

"Sorry, Shep," Snoop grunted. "I-was-only-trying-to-open-the-doors-like-you-said-do-you-think-this-means-we're-trapped —"

"Trapped?" barked Rufus. "Did he say trapped?"

"No!" Shep snarled. "No one's trapped." *If these yappers would shut their jowls for a* heartbeat . . . "We just need to hit this tree harder."

Regaining his stance, Shep reared to hit the tree again with his paws. Virgil joined him and they lunged against the trunk together. Their combined weight knocked the tree over. It banged into the glass and lodged in the cracks of the web. The glass bulged out, but would not break.

All the dogs started to howl at once — they *were* trapped! Even Shep felt the claws of fear scratching at his heart.

Callie appeared from down the hall toward Higgins's den. "I found a way out!" she barked. "There's a door down here that smells like Outside!"

"Let me smell!" Shep leapt over the small dogs at his paws, and he and Callie raced down the hall ahead of the pack.

"Good find," Shep barked as they ran. He was a little annoyed that she hadn't mentioned this door *before* he started with the tree.

Callie must have sensed it, because she glanced at Shep, her head lowered apologetically. "I'm sorry I didn't say anything. I just figured that, with how nervous the pack was, I should start looking for another way Out on the sneak, in case the glass didn't break."

They stopped in front of a door.

Callie snorted, head down and ears floppy. "I didn't mean to show you up in there. You had a good idea."

"I was following your old idea," Shep woofed. He flicked his tail and panted, grinning. It was hard to stay mad at Callie.

"We're a good team," she replied, tail wagging and eyes bright.

Shep sniffed the door and drew in the scents of Outside. This door had a metal bar across its middle, like the door in the stairwell. *Thank the Great Wolf!*

Shep slapped the bar with his paws and pushed the door open, then stood against it, holding it open for the rest of the dogs. They scrambled Outside into the alley — even Boji managed to hop over the doorway without too much "Oh, dear"-ing.

Only Dover gave Shep a wag of thanks as he passed. "You're doing good," the old timer woofed.

It surprised Shep how much that kibble of support meant to him. "Thanks," he managed to yip back.


The alley was not large, barely two stretches wide and filled with Car-sized square metal bins and piles of shiny black bags. A palm frond three stretches long was wedged against the brick wall not far from where Shep stood. Puddles of rainwater, some infected with shimmering chemicals, covered most of the ground, meaning every dog's paws were soaked. The small dogs, especially Ginny with her long coat, were drenched to their bellies. Oscar avoided drowning by climbing on top of a black bag.

From Outside, Shep could see that the dogs' building was not the only one to have been crushed by the storm. The sunrise side of the building across the street was gone; nothing but a pile of rubble remained. The opposite wall of the alley ended three floors up, but a skeleton of pipes rose several stretches above the jagged edge of the brick.

The weather, however, frightened Shep more than the broken buildings. Although he could hear rain falling all around and thunder rumbling in the clouds, the sky was clear above the alley. The air was thick with water and still as a stone, though winds roared nearby and shifting air currents twitched his whiskers. The storm had them surrounded.

"What do we do now?" Rufus whined.

The dogs, who were huddled in several groups, instantly looked at Shep. They seemed to be waiting for him to woof, like he was their leader. Paws soaked and fur trembling, they all seemed to have forgotten the very idea that pestered Shep like a flea: the fact that he had no clue what he was doing, that he was not supposed to be rescuing dogs, but rather home in his den waiting for his boy — assuming he still had a den to return to.

A chorus of yapping commenced: "Yeah, it smells like more rain's coming." "We'll be soaked!" "We should never have left our dens!" "Where's my mistress?" "What should we do, Shep?" "Yeah, Shep?" "SHEP!" His name rang in his ears as the dogs began howling it in unison.

Zeus appeared beside Shep. His ears pricked forward and his eyes widened. He panted hard. "What have you become, Shep?" Zeus said, his bark dripping with sarcasm. "King of the Yappers?" He nipped Shep's mane, then trotted over to a pile of bags and began pawing at them.

Shep wanted to join him. He was hungry and exhausted. He felt like he'd been awake for cycles. He needed a good meal and a soft bed and rest for the next several moons. He had no idea what to do. Why was he here, again? Why did he rescue all these whiny little yappers in the first place? All they did was complain!

"We have to find a new den before the storm returns," Callie said. She sat beside Shep, ears twitching. She trembled.

Shep wanted to make her happy, to keep her safe. He liked being a part of her team. But he was so tired.

"I know a place," yipped Ginny. "My mistress takes me to this bright den filled with kibble and soft beds and treats and toys. I get my fur cleaned there by professionals," she woofed, snout in the air.

"There's no place like that," snapped Zeus. "Humans would never make such a place."

"I've been there, too," growled Daisy. She thrust out her bulky chest and strutted up to Zeus. "Ginny's — *snort* — telling the truth, so back off."

She had no fear, that Daisy. Shep hoped Zeus would

stay calm — he didn't have enough energy to break up a fight.

Zeus snarled at Daisy, then shifted his stance. "You deal with the yappers," he grunted to Shep. He shoved Daisy out of his way as he passed to resume his investigation of the black bags.

Callie watched Zeus leave and sighed with relief. "Chew my rawhide! You dogs seem to sniff out reasons to growl at each other. Ginny, I think that's a brilliant idea. How do we get there?"

The whole mess of dogs pressed close to Callie and Ginny, sniffing and rolling and yipping and panting, and ignored Shep. He groaned with happiness at the loss of their attention.

# CHAPTER 10
## HAVEN

Ginny trotted out into the street with Callie at her side, and the other dogs raced to follow them. Shep, on the other paw, could barely maintain his loping stride, and he lagged behind the pack. His jaws hurt, and his paws hurt, and he thought maybe he'd injured a shoulder slamming into that indoor tree.

Nearby, Boji carried little Oscar in her jaws. The pup hadn't spoken to Shep since Daisy told him about Shep's "lie." Shep hadn't known the pup was from a store. Shep wasn't even sure what it meant to come from the store, as if a dog were a bag of kibble. He'd only been trying to help when he'd promised to find Oscar's dam, to get the little dog to move out of the dark. It began to seem to Shep that the more he helped, the more trouble he fell into. Sure, he felt good having freed these dogs, having saved Callie from the grate and the attack bird, but he was also tired of their whining, of the responsibility of keeping them all safe. He wanted to go home. He wanted his own bed. He wanted to be taken care of. He wanted his boy.

Zeus appeared at his side. "Now we're following the yappers?" he growled. "What's next? The big dogs wait while they get first choice of the kibble?"

"Great Wolf, Zeus," Shep groaned. "Lay off with the yapper stuff, okay?"

"Whoa," he snarled. "Look who's got a burr in his fur."

Shep sighed and licked his jowls. "I don't have a burr in my fur. I've been up all night, I'm hungry, and I'm sick of being yapped at."

"Who's yapping?" Zeus growled. "You calling me a yapper?"

Shep snorted loudly, then bounded away from his friend. He just wanted to be left alone.

Ginny, followed by Callie and now Frizzle, led the dogs toward sunrise. The street was littered with glass from broken windows and shards of wood and plastic of all colors. Soggy paper clumped in the gutters. Once, a rat darted out from an opening, only to scurry just as quickly back into the dark.

Wary of these empty streets, the dogs moved in a tight pack. Daisy lagged behind the rest, huffing and snorting in the humidity. Shep fell in near her at the rear, on the fringe.

He scented the air. The winds were confusing; first they blew from sunset, then from sunrise. It seemed that the storm wasn't sure if it wanted to head one way or the other. Rain dripped down in fat drops for a few heart-beats, then stopped. Clouds were bunched in the sky above them like kicked-up bedding. The scent of storm whirled around Shep, masking the smells of everything else. Not that Shep could have fought off so much as a hungry tabby should anything attack: That was how exhausted he was feeling.

Shep was grateful that the streets were empty. The dogs were far too small a pack for Shep to feel safe. And even if he'd rescued more, these dogs were all pets; they'd never had to protect themselves from anything more than an advancing floor-sucker. Though Shep himself had battled the floor-sucker many times, it did not compare to what it took to battle the likes of Kaz.

He shivered at the thought of the wild dog. When they'd fought in the Park, she'd been fierce, but worse than that, she'd been fearless. She attacked Shep with no thought as to whether she'd survive the battle. She seemed unaware of the danger he posed, or else — and this frightened him even more — she didn't care. It was as if she were entirely possessed by the Black Dog, like she was the Black Dog himself. Shep had never met a dog who was so thoroughly wild. At least in the fight cage, his opponents had wanted to live as much as he did; a fighter knew what to expect from a dog whose only thought was survival. But to fight a dog who cared nothing for her own life, who fought simply for the joy of her own destruction . . .

Shep pushed these thoughts from his mind. The streets were clear. He did not see a bird in the sky or an iguana in a tree. Everything had sought some shelter from the storm. And he was no longer the leader — Ginny was. Let her figure something out.

"It's not far now!" bellowed Ginny. She bustled ahead, moving as quickly as her dainty paws could carry her.

Callie raced beside her, ears up and tail swinging. Frizzle was not far behind, his wing-ears sticking up like flags and waving with each jaunty stride. The others huddled close as they trotted along, glancing warily at the scene around them. Shep recalled how wretched he'd felt when he first left his den. Part of him wanted to bark a woof of encouragement, but then he saw Zeus loping along at the edge of the group and thought better of it. *I am* not *the King of the Yappers.*

Ginny stopped at a building, the front of which was covered in sheets of wood.

"Where're the piles of kib, yapper?" Zeus growled. "Where're the endless rows of beds?"

Ginny whimpered, sniffing at the wood in one place, then trotting to another piece and sniffing there. "I can smell the kibble," she yipped. "This wood isn't normally here, I tell you. Would that dear old Lassie were here to save us!"

The other dogs began to whimper and whine. Their fear smell wafted into the air, rivaling the stench of the storm.

"Well, Lassie isn't here," barked Callie, "so we have to pull the wood off ourselves. Shep!"

He winced at the sound of his name, then lumbered to her side. Shep shook himself to try to wake up. His eyelids drooped and his legs trembled from exhaustion.

"Can you bite that corner of wood?" Callie asked. "If you can, you could pull the plank off the wall."

Shep sighed, then sniffed at the corner of the wood. He made a few attempts to dig his teeth into the pulp, but couldn't get a bite.

"It won't work," he said, finally. "It's too close to the wall to get a good hold with my teeth."

Callie snorted, then began to sniff around for another solution. The winds began to pick up from sunrise, bringing with them the strong salt scent of the ocean. Fat raindrops began to fall.

"We should head back," grumbled Rufus, the square-dog. He winced at the tap of each drop of rain on his fur. "We should never have left our dens," he moaned.

Frizzle stalked over to the square, gray naysayer. "Hey, dog," he woofed. "Don't grumble. Callie will figure something out."

Rufus snorted. "Then what? We'll all be torn apart when the storm comes. And don't call me 'dog' — the name's Rufus."

"Don't be such a tail dragger, *Rufus*," Frizzle snapped, cuffing the squaredog on the scruff with his fangs. "You're bringing the whole pack down."

Rufus growled, but kept his jowls shut. Frizzle strutted through the crowd of dogs, yapping, "No grumbling! If it wasn't for Callie, you'd all be stuck in the dark with the ceiling crushing your mangy muzzles!"

Callie snuffled along the wall of wood, sniffing each plank, then pawing at its edges. She stopped in front of one plank and reared against it. She pushed on it a few times and it groaned. She jumped back, cringing. But nothing happened.

"What are you doing?" yipped Frizzle. "Can I help?"

"This plank is loose," Callie woofed. "I think if we push on it, it might fall off."

Shep had no idea where she came up with this stuff. He trotted up to the plank and nosed his way between Frizzle and the wall.

"This is a job for a big dog," he barked. He began thrusting his front paws against the plank.

"Wait!" howled Callie.

The plank squealed, then slid down the wall with a crash, slamming straight onto Dover's tail.

The old-timer shrieked with pain and scrambled away from the wood, but was held back by his trapped tail. Shep was horrified. He began digging at the plank.

"We have to push on the wood!" Callie barked.

Virgil and Cheese shoved past Shep and jumped onto the plank. The force of their bodies lifted the wood just enough for Dover to free his tail.

Dover waddled a few stretches into the street, then sat and licked his wound. Boji and Ginny joined him, sniffing and licking him all over. Every few heartbeats, one would look at Shep like he'd just torn the squeaker from their favorite toy.

"Nice one, Big Nose," Frizzle yapped, panting, his mouth open wide, splitting his head nearly in two.

Shep skulked away from the wall, out to the edge of the pack. He crossed the Sidewalk and sat in a patch of muddy grass. He'd hurt a dog, an old-timer at that. He'd only been trying to help. Wasn't that what they wanted, his help? Wasn't he the rescuer? The big dog?

Zeus sidled up to Shep and sat beside him, flank to flank. "See?" Zeus snarled. "You try to do something nice and you get bitten. Stay on the sidelines, brother." He licked his jowls. "You stick your nose into the rat's nest and you're bound to get scratched."

Dark clouds scudded overhead; thick rain fell like spittle from the Black Dog's jowls. Callie remained by the plank, sniffing and pawing at its edges. She peered behind the wood and stuck her snout between it and the wall. The topmost sliver of a wall of glass peeked out from behind the plank.

Frizzle sat on his haunches near Callie, head cocked, staring at her. "We could hit the wood again," he yapped. "See what happens."

"My thought exactly," Callie yipped. "I think if we push on the wood some more, the plank might break the clear stuff. It's already cracked near one of the corners."

She wasn't barking to Shep this time; she was barking to Virgil and Cheese. She didn't even look at Shep as she explained exactly how she wanted them to push on the plank. It was like she didn't want his help anymore.

Shep watched as Cheese and Virgil jumped against Callie's plank. The wood wobbled and banged against the glass, which began to crunch. The winds helped, pulling on the wood as it bounced from each push of the dogs' paws. Virgil and Cheese gave the plank a final slam, and the glass shattered. The wood shrieked and fell toward the wall. The dogs scrambled out of the way. The plank crashed through the window, showering the street with bits of glass, then came to rest.

The plank was now like a wooden tongue protruding from a snarling maw lined with clear fangs. Its bottom lay on the Sidewalk, and the length of it extended through what remained of the window into the building. Rainwater trailed down its surface like slobber.

Callie stepped out of the crowd of trembling dogs and padded up to the plank. "I think it's stopped," she woofed. Just then, the wind whirled and rattled the plank; the wood shivered against the Sidewalk, but stayed in place.

"That's my girldog!" howled Frizzle. "She doesn't just bust down the wall, she smashes the window and makes a ramp for us all to get inside." He licked Callie's nose and she squealed with delight.

Frizzle stood beside Callie like a proud sire — as if he had anything to do with her plan's success. But maybe he did. Maybe Frizzle was Callie's new partner. Maybe Shep was no longer needed on her team.

A gust of wind that felt like it could tear fur from flesh blasted the pack, smacking their pelts with raindrops.

"We have to get inside!" Callie bellowed. She hopped onto the bottom of the plank and trotted up toward the broken window; the plank wobbled, but remained in place. She stopped just inside the hole and scented the air.

"Is it safe?" asked Boji, sniffing gingerly at the bottom of the plank.

"Is there kibble?" yapped Rufus.

"Yes!" barked Callie, looking over her tail at them. "And yes!" Then she leapt off the wood into the darkness.

"Callie!" Frizzle yowled. He raced up the ramp and dove into the dark after her.

The rest of the pack hesitated at the bottom of the wooden tongue. The rain fell in a torrent; Shep was once again soaked to the skin. Some of the smaller dogs began to whine.

"It's amazing!"

Frizzle's shrill bark whistled out of the hole. They were alive! They'd survived! There was kibble! Suddenly, all the dogs were clamoring to get inside. Even Boji scrabbled up the creaking plank, belly to wood, all fears forgotten.

"I'm going in," Zeus barked. He pushed his way through the crowd of dogs. "I call dibs on first choice of kibble!" he howled.

Shep waited, not wanting to get any more nasty looks from the other dogs. After every other dog was inside, Shep loped his soggy, sore body up the ramp.

The plank led into a huge, dark space. By the smell of it, Shep figured it was a hundred stretches in every direction. Above the sunrise half of the main floor, there was an open balcony that smelled strongly of rodent. Bright lights glared from the walls like those that had come on in the hallways of the den-building. They dimly lit row after row of tall shelves, which, from the rustling sound echoing throughout the space, stored bags and bags of kibble. Howls of joy rose up from all around Shep.

Zeus bounded over to his side, mouth full of jerky

treats. "It's incredible! Treats! Everywhere, there's treats!" He barked and frisked about like a pup, then raced into one of the rows lined with squeaky toys.

Shep scented out a row filled with bags of kibble and tore into the nearest one. Just as he swallowed his first delicious mouthful, he heard the scritch of claws on the stone floor behind him.

"I've been looking for you!" yapped Callie. "We need to get the pack organized. The others are running around like beetles under a rock." She wagged her tail and held her head high, friendly.

"What do you need me for?" Shep grumbled, scooping a second bite into his jaws. "I thought Frizzle was helping you."

"Frizzle? Yes, but what's that got to do with anything?" She hopped onto the bag of kibble so she could look Shep in the eyes. "You seemed upset after what happened with Dover, so I asked the other dogs for help. Was I wrong?" She cocked her head. Her jowls were caught on both of her bottom fangs, giving her the silliest expression, though Shep knew she was being serious. Her eyes were deep and warm and curious. "What's the matter with you?" she woofed.

"Nothing," Shep growled, turning away from her and tearing into a different bag. "Just leave me alone. I'm sick of taking care of this pack of yappers. I'm hungry and tired and just want to get back to my den."

Callie snorted and jumped onto this new bag. Her ears lay against her head and her tail was tucked low. "Fine, Shep," she growled. "See this?" She jumped off the bag and turned her rump toward him. "This is me leaving you alone." She loped stiff-legged out of the aisle and into the dark beyond.

Shep could hardly swallow the kibbles down. His throat felt dry and tight.

"Who needs you, anyway," he grumbled. He spat out what food remained in his jaws and smelled for an aisle that contained beds. Gripping his teeth around the biggest bed he found, he dragged a whole pile down on top of his back. He dug his way to the top of the pile, circled once, twice, and then flopped down, falling instantly into a deep sleep.

# CHAPTER 11
## THE FLASH OF LIGHTNING

Screams and shrieks echoed around him. Harsh barks, whimpers, claws scraping on stone, the anxious chattering of teeth: All rang throughout the cavernous space. At first, Shep thought he was dreaming. But he was not. He'd been woken from his first-ever dreamless sleep. Blinking his eyes to adjust them to the dark, he dragged his tired bones up from the pile of bedding he'd made for himself.

"I said *get out*!" The bark was loud and sharp, and unmistakably Frizzle's.

Shep trotted to the end of the aisle, ears up and nose ready. It smelled like near midsun, but only dim light and a mist of rainwater poured in through the hole in the window made by Callie's ramp. In that gray space stood Frizzle, with Callie and Higgins not far behind, their hackles raised and trembling. Facing Frizzle were three beastly dogs: one white, one black, and one dusky tan with a pink nose. Slobber dripped from their exposed fangs and trembling jowls. They smelled of human garbage and dirt — wild dogs.

"This is *our* den," growled Frizzle. "We found it, and you're not taking it!"

"Frizzle, no!" howled Shep.

Shep sprang toward them, fangs bared, paw pads splaying for better grip on the smooth floor. But he was too late.

The white wild dog lashed forward and caught Frizzle around the neck. Frizzle yelped as he was flung high into the air, clamped in the big dog's jaws. The white dog landed hard on stiff legs and threw Frizzle across the floor with a flick of his head. Frizzle's little body flopped against the stone, then slid on the smooth surface, turning slightly before coming to rest against a shelf.

Shep's heart raced, lifeblood pounding through his veins and ringing in his ears. He shot into the air and crashed like a wave onto the white dog's neck. His fangs ripped into the white fur and his jaws locked. The wild dog howled and shook his head. He rolled onto his side and began to slash at Shep with his claws.

Shep raked the dog's belly with his own claws, then released his jaws and sprang away. The white flipped over and onto his paws. They circled one another, jowls trembling, fangs bared.

"So these pets have a guard dog," growled the white, head low and ears flat.

"You leave them alone," spat Shep, hackles bristling along his back like flames.

"Here's the deal," the white said, tongue flickering between dripping fangs. "You die, and then we tear these stinking pets to shreds, one by one, until they go back to their dens."

The dog leapt high, but kept his head low, catching his fangs on Shep's collar. Then he jerked his muzzle, choking Shep.

Shep squealed and his tongue flopped from his mouth. He'd forgotten about the collar. He ducked his head and pulled back. The collar slipped off; it hung limp from the wild dog's jowls. The last piece of his boy had been taken from him.

"I've got your collar," the white dog snarled, spitting the fabric loop out onto the floor. "Guess that means you're my pet now?" The other two wild dogs moved closer, hackles bristled, fangs bared, whiplike tails flat and trembling.

"I have a deal for you," growled Shep. "The deal is you leave and never come back." He leapt off his hind legs and caught the white dog under his jaw. Shep rolled, dragging the white onto his side.

With a yelp, the wild dog fell hard on his back. The impact knocked Shep's jaws from their hold on the fur. Shep rolled out of the way, sprang to his paws, and resumed his stance, ready for the next attack.

The white scrambled back, joining his two pack-mates. He was panting hard. Red lifeblood stained the fur around his neck.

The wild dog glared at the other dogs, the pets, who cowered in the dark. "I'll be back with the rest of our pack. You have until then to clear out." He spat ruddy drool at Shep's paws. "I doubt you can protect them all."

The three wild dogs backed away from Shep, then leapt onto the wood ramp and raced out into the storm.

Shep nosed his collar where it lay in a pool of lifeblood and slobber. *Good-bye, Boy.* He took a deep, shuddering breath, then snorted and turned to the other dogs. They were pressed against the nearby shelves, paralyzed with fear. Even the bigger dogs like Cheese and Virgil trembled under their fur.

Zeus emerged from the dark of one of the aisles. "Let's get out of here," he woofed to Shep. "If we go now, we can catch up with those dogs and work out a truce."

"They're wild dogs, Zeus," Shep grunted. "They're not going to bargain with small dogs."

"Who said anything about small dogs?" Zeus stood, tail stiff, ears flat. "You're not telling me you're staying with these yappers?"

Shep cocked his head. "Of course I'm staying," he barked. "Aren't you?"

Zeus backed away, toward the hole. "I'm going where I know I'll be safe," he growled. "With the other big dogs." Rain blasted by the winds spattered the floor at his paws.

"Don't go," Shep said, stepping toward his friend, tail low and wagging. "We need you. I need you. I can't protect them all myself."

"So leave," Zeus snapped. "Come with me. We'll go off, just the two of us. We can protect ourselves." His stub tail bobbed and his ears flicked forward.

"I can't leave them," Shep snuffled, glancing back at the huddled shadows of the other dogs. "They're defenseless."

"You're one paw in the hole," Zeus spat. "They're already four paws in it, and you're willingly stepping into that hole with them." He sprang onto the wooden ramp. "It's your lifeblood that's going to be spilt," he barked. "And for what? A couple of yappers."

Zeus bounded down the plank and into the whirling rain. Lightning flashed, sparkling along Zeus's coat, and then all was dark. Zeus was gone.

A howl rose from behind Shep, near the shelves. It was Callie's clear voice, and it sounded out her broken heart. Her paws rested beside the motionless black fur of Frizzle's back. Red lifeblood pooled around her claws.

Shep loped to her side and sat behind her. "I'm sorry," he woofed softly.

"You were right about the wild dogs," she said. Her bark was flat and cold. "They were terrible. Those three bounded in over the plank and started nosing the other dogs around, barking that they claimed this den and all the kibble. Only Frizzle had the fur to stand up to them." Callie gently licked Frizzle's hide. "Now look at him."

"If I'd been with you instead of sulking alone, I could have protected you — him." Shep whimpered, crouching low, and rested his head beside Callie's flank. His nose filled with the sickening scent of spilt lifeblood.

"I saw Zeus leave," Callie woofed. "Why didn't you go with him? You must know that when those wild dogs come back, we'll be torn apart like toys."

Shep sighed. "Remember that legend I was telling you before the bird attacked, the one about the Great Wolf?"

Callie glanced at Shep, then returned her gaze to Frizzle's body.

"I never got to tell you the ending."

*The pup snarled and spat in front of the huge paws of the Great Wolf. All dogs heard his challenge and came running to see what the Great Wolf would do.*

*The Great Wolf looked down at the pup, whose eyes flashed with brazen fury. The Great Wolf bowed his head, acknowledging the challenge, and the pup attacked. He dug his tiny teeth into the Great Wolf's hide, and scratched his sharp claws at the thick fur. All dogs waited for the Great Wolf to deal the death blow to the pup. Dams whimpered, dragging their own pups to their sides.*

*The Great Wolf, however, rolled away from the pup. He sprang far back, and then leapt off of the mountain. The Great Wolf could not bring himself to kill the innocent pup, and so he sacrificed himself. He tumbled down, nose over tail, the cold wind ruffling his fur, and for the first time, he felt peace.*

*All dogs howled with grief, including the pup, who had realized, too late, what he'd done.*

*The Silver Moon heard their cries. She reached out and caught the Great Wolf before he hit the ground. She carried him into the sky, and the Great Wolf grew, covering the world.*

*"You will be my companion," the Silver Moon said, "and help me to watch over all dogs as long as I shine down upon them."*

*The Great Wolf curled his huge body around the Silver Moon. The moonstuff glinted off every hair in his coat like tiny fires across the sky. Below, the dogs marveled at how he sparkled throughout the night.*

"That story changed everything for me," Shep woofed. "I wanted to live as much as the next dog, but I realized that the cruelty of the fight kennel wasn't the only way. I tried to kill my opponent as quickly as possible, without causing much pain. I would peek through the walls of the kennel at night and see those sparkling lights in the sky and hope that when the Great Wolf looked down on me, he saw that I was a good dog."

Callie had curled herself into a tight ball against Frizzle's back as she listened to Shep's story. When he finished, she opened her eyes.

"The point is," Shep said, "I don't think it's every dog for himself. I think we're meant to stick together, big dogs and small." Shep sat up. "I just wish I'd been there. I wish it'd been me facing off with the wild dogs and not Frizzle."

"He wouldn't have wanted that," Callie said. "Even if you'd been there, he would've done the same thing." Callie nuzzled Frizzle's fur. "Stupid mutt."

"He was a brave dog," Shep woofed. "A pain in the tail, but a brave one."

Callie panted softly. "You're a good packmate," she yipped. "Frizzle knew that. I know that."

"We all — *snort* — know it," barked Daisy.

While Shep had been telling his story, the other dogs had huddled around him. They all looked at him now with big eyes, tails low and wagging, ears forward, waiting to hear what he had to howl. And this time, it didn't feel like a burden. Shep realized that to these dogs, he was the Great Wolf, the defender of the peace. That wasn't a burden — that was a gift.

# CHAPTER 12
## WINDS RISING

Thunder crashed, shaking the whole building to the very floor the dogs stood on. Oscar yowled miserably and Boji licked his head several times. Shep could see that all the dogs were nervous, and that they were waiting for him to bark.

"We should go back to our dens," he snuffled.

"What'd he woof?" barked Rufus, who stood at the far edge of the pack. "I can't hear anything back here! Did he bark that we should go home? I've been barking about that for heartbeats!"

Daisy strutted up to Rufus and nipped him on the jowl. "Look Outside," she snapped. "Think you can paw it — *snort* — home in that?"

Every dog looked out the hole in the window.

The clouds above them were black, though Shep knew it should still be light out. The wind howled like the Black Dog himself and sheets of rain tore leaves from the nearby trees. Every few heartbeats, thunder grumbled and the sky blazed with lightning.

"We can't go Outside," Callie moaned, trembling as the clouds flashed white. "We'll be washed away."

Shep did not disagree, but he couldn't think of another plan. He wasn't a planner — he was a doer. Callie was the one who thought of stuff. Shep looked at the little girldog. Her whole body slumped toward Frizzle's silent form. Now *there* was a situation he could do something about.

"Wherever we decide to go, we can't leave Frizzle here," Shep woofed. "Let's give him a proper burial."

Callie flapped her curled tail. "Where can we bury him?" she asked. "Outside is too dangerous, and there are no holes in here."

When he died, Shep wanted to be carried like the Great Wolf into the sky. However, Shep was not the Silver Moon; he couldn't carry Frizzle that far. But he knew of someplace high up and wonderfully soft that might feel like a cloud.

"I have the perfect place," Shep barked.

He lifted Frizzle's body gently in his mouth, holding him like he had little Oscar, between his teeth. He loped into the darkness, back down the aisles between the tall shelves, until he came to the tower of bedding that he'd made for himself. He climbed up onto the mound, a stretch above the floor, and rested Frizzle's body in the center of all the beds. Closing his eyes, Shep dragged a large bed over the body.

The other dogs had followed Callie and him and now surrounded the pile of bedding.

"Shouldn't some dog say something?" Boji asked.

Higgins stood and snorted. "He was a good chap, Frizzle," he began. "He was a scrapper, and liked kibble, and girldogs." Higgins coughed and ran his paw over his nose. "Oh, hang it, I'm terrible with speeches."

"No," Shep woofed. "That was . . . nice."

The dogs snuffled their agreement. Only Callie stared into the velvet skin of the bed in front of her, her tail beneath her slumped haunches. She needed more than that.

*Frizzle deserves more than that.*

Shep looked at the bed he'd placed over the body. "When I was a pup," he woofed, "I fought other dogs to survive. I hated it, but worse than the fighting was what they did with the dog who lost. The humans would just toss the body into a hole. Just like that, without so much as a stroke on the ears."

Shep licked his jowls, then continued. "A fight dog deserves more — all dogs do. But now, I'm barking about a fight dog. A dog who wasn't afraid to stand up to three dogs at once. Three dogs who were bigger than he was and more vicious than anything you've ever seen." Shep rested a paw on the bed covering Frizzle. "I under-estimated you," he woofed. "You, Frizzle, were an amazing fighter. Thank you for defending us."

Callie keened. Her cry rose like the Silver Moon and resounded throughout the den. One by one, the others joined her until the whole building echoed with their voices.

*Great Wolf, watch over him.* Shep joined their cry.


The echoes quieted until all that remained were the howling winds and pounding rain of the storm. The dogs looked up at Shep, their ears forward and tails wagging. Even Callie looked to him. In that heartbeat, Shep felt what the Great Wolf must have felt — the pressure to make things right. But he was not the Great Wolf; he was just a regular dog. Fear dug its claws into his heart. He could not lead them alone.

Shep leapt down off the pile of bedding, landing between Rufus and Cheese. The dogs became confused — wasn't Shep the alpha? Whimpers and soft cries echoed throughout the space, and the dogs chattered their teeth anxiously.

"We need to work together," Shep barked. "I can't defend you myself."

The whimpers grew louder.

"But I can help you defend yourselves," he howled. "Higgins, Ginny, you both know about human things. Is there anything here we can use to keep the wild dogs from attacking? Callie, do you have any ideas?"

"You were on the right scent before," snapped Rufus. "We clear out of this place and head back to our dens before those mongrels return."

Several dogs moaned their agreement. Callie remained silent, her eyes on the burial mound. Shep smelled the pack's fear growing. Rufus's yapping wasn't helping.

"Remember what this storm did to your dens?" Shep barked. "We can't run away from the wild dogs; we have nowhere else to go."

The fear scent bloomed until it overwhelmed Shep's

nose. Oscar cowered beneath Boji's belly. Ginny paced and mumbled about a potential rescue by Lassie. Even easygoing Cheese wagged his tail harder and panted heavy breaths.

Perhaps his focus on the den-destroying storm wasn't helping, either.

"You're all strong, healthy dogs," Shep began, trying a new track. "We can defend this den from an attack." Shep glanced quickly around the space in front of him. "There," he barked. "If the smaller dogs get on top of those shelves, they'll be safe from danger. And the big dogs can drop down on the wild dogs and gain an attack advantage."

"Excuse me," yapped Higgins. He shuffled out from the mess of dogs. "What if instead of dropping themselves onto the wild dogs, the dogs dropped the objects from the shelves onto them? The wild dogs would never expect that. It might scare the scoundrels off." His tiny tail wiggled and his ears pricked forward.

"Brilliant!" yipped Callie. Shep could see that she was shaking off the sadness like rain from her fur. "What else can we do?" She wagged her tail excitedly, jaws open and eyes bright.

Shep felt stronger with Callie beside him. "What about this thing?" he woofed. He loped over to a clear tank full of water with little flickering things swimming inside it. "If we pulled this over, it might scare the wild dogs."

Callie sniffed the base of the tank. "Smells good to me."

The other dogs stood taller, and their tails began to wag. It was working!

"The wild dogs won't expect us to defend ourselves," Shep barked, his voice strong. "If we do anything besides cower with our tails between our legs, they'll be shaken. Daisy," he yipped, nipping her shoulder, "you're made of some tough fur. What ideas do you have?"

Daisy's bug eyes bulged ever farther out of her head. "Me? Well, let's see." She snuffled around, ending up at the ramp. "What about this?" she yapped. "If we nudge the plank out of the hole, the wild dogs will have a tough time getting inside."

"Double brilliant!" squealed Callie. She was practically hopping around the den. "Yes! Cheese, any big dog — if you lift this end of the plank with your head, it should slide Outside."

Rufus pushed his way to the front. "But if we get rid of the plank, how will we escape? We'll be trapped!" His eyes were wide. Shep sensed that fear had its fangs around Rufus's neck.

"Don't worry," Shep assured him. His deep, grumbling voice both soothed and cowed the anxious squaredog. "Once we've defended this place from the wild dogs, and once the storm has blown away, we'll figure something out." He stood over Rufus, eyes hard and steady, ears forward and tail high.

Rufus understood — Shep was in charge, but he wasn't going to bully Rufus into submission. Rufus bowed his head. "There's a second level above this one." He sighed. "Perhaps those of us who are no good for anything can simply cower up there?"

Callie strutted up to Rufus and nipped him on the neck — she'd learned a thing or two from Frizzle. "Enough of this tail-dragger talk! Every dog is good for something! Your idea is actually helpful, Rufus. That second floor will be our backup plan. If the wild dogs get too far inside, we'll all run for the second floor and hide there."

Rufus's eyes glinted and his jaws opened in a light pant. "You like my idea?" he snuffled.

"It's a great idea," Callie woofed. "Now let's all get to work!"

\*     \*     \*

Shep gratefully handed over the role of leader to Callie and Higgins. They began barking orders and the other dogs followed their commands. Callie had Virgil and Cheese work on pushing the ramp out of the hole in the window.

Higgins had an idea for how to get the small dogs on top of the shelf. "What if you big chaps knock this other shelf over?" he yapped, indicating the shelf next to the one Shep had pointed out for the aerial attack. "Then we can climb up it, the way we used the wooden plank to get inside here."

Snoop and Dover joined Shep, and the three began to push on the shelf. After a few thrusts with their fore-paws, the shelf began to wobble.

As he watched, Higgins spouted more uses for his shelf-ramp. "From the top of the shelf," he barked, "we can get up onto the second level without having to leg it to the stairs at the back of the den. And as we run up the ramp-shelf, we can also drag toys and other things up with us to drop onto the wild dogs."

"Sounds good," woofed Shep, though he had a hard time keeping up with the little Furface's chatter.

Once Higgins's ramp was in place, Shep bounded from site to site, lending a paw or a fang to whatever else needed doing. Boji was sniffing out a way to topple over the tank full of water. She found a handle on the front, but pointed out that the tank would then fall onto whoever pulled the handle.

"Oh, dear," she woofed. "And I do hate doors. But what if I just pushed it from the back?" She trotted around to the back of the cabinet and, rearing, slammed her forepaws into the tank. It wobbled!

The more the dogs snuffled about, the more ideas they had. Callie dragged beds from the aisle where they'd buried Frizzle to cover the sharp, clear teeth on the floor around the window. That way, the big dogs could push the ramp out without hurting their paws.

"And after, we can pull the beds off to give the wild dogs a nasty surprise," Callie barked, a wicked glimmer in her eye.

Even Oscar had an idea. "They're coming here because they're hungry, right?" he yipped. "What if we tear open some bags of kibble? They might run to eat it instead of attacking us."

Shep was so happy, he rolled the little pup with a playful slap of the snout. Oscar panted, scrambled to his paws, and pounced on Shep's tail. Shep rolled onto his side, allowing the pup to jump on top of him.

"You got me!" Shep cried.

Oscar's tail wagged so hard that he fell over and rolled off Shep's belly.

They played for a few heartbeats, and then Oscar stepped back.

"Thanks," he woofed.

"What for?" Shep rolled onto his paws.

"For saving me up in that hallway," Oscar said. "But you didn't have to say you'd find my mom."

"You were pretty scared," Shep woofed. He'd kind of hoped the pup had forgotten the whole morning.

"Yes," Oscar yipped. "But you smell like a good dog. I'd follow you anywhere." The pup licked Shep on the nose, then bounded away calling for Boji and yapping about his kibble idea.

There was a loud crash. Shep scrambled down the aisle and saw that the others had succeeded in pushing the plank out of the window. Callie began dragging the beds off the fangs of broken glass. Shep joined her.

"Good idea," he woofed. "The wild dogs will get a bite on the paw when they first step inside. Maybe it'll keep some of them from jumping through the hole."

"I thought the wild dogs would follow their alpha anywhere," barked Callie.

"Maybe not," Shep replied. "Some are loyal to the pack leader, but many are just scavengers. They follow the pack when it suits them. If a couple of dogs cut a paw jumping in here, the rest might think twice about following."

Callie dropped the bed by the side of a shelf. "How do you know so much about these wild dogs?"

The woofs solidified on his tongue. *What will Callie think of me?*

"I was one."

One night in the fight kennels, Shep was awoken by the shriek of a siren. All the dogs began to howl. The kennel doors burst open and strange men in dark clothes, with shiny black bowls on their heads and blinding lights in their hands, charged in. Some had guns and they began shooting dogs with darts; others had long poles with ropes dangling from them.

The fear smell was so thick Shep gagged with each breath. He knew something bad was happening. When a man in black cut open the lock on his cage, Shep bolted for the door. He knocked the man over and raced down the path between the cages, claws scraping the stone. There was so much noise and confusion, so many dogs howling and thrashing in their cages, that Shep was able to slip out of the kennel doors and into the dark.

Outside, he was confronted with strange smells and noises. The dirt, the trees, everything was new to a pup born in a stone cage with metal mesh walls. Shep stumbled over roots and slogged through mud, scenting for anything familiar. Smells of gasoline and human sweat led him out of the woods and onto a street lined with boxy human dens. The Silver Moon hung above him with the Great Wolf's coat glinting all around her. Shep begged the Great Wolf for help.

And suddenly, help appeared.

A lean brown dog toppled over a garbage can and nosed around in the refuse looking for kibble.

Shep approached in a low crouch, ears up and nose open, tail flat. He didn't want to appear aggressive, but he wasn't going to be caught off guard. He grumbled a greeting, with the slightest note of warning mixed into his bark.

The other dog looked at him briefly, then went back to nosing through the trash. His tail remained flat and he didn't raise his hackles. He seemed to be inviting Shep to join him, and so Shep loped a bit closer. Shep flicked his tail, asking if he could sniff; the strange dog wagged his tail back and made no move to attack. Shep scented the dog's rump: He was older then Shep, but not an old timer; he wasn't hungry, but wasn't rolling in kibble; and he had no scent of human anywhere on him.

"Where are you from?" Shep yipped, still keeping his distance.

"From?" the dog barked. "Everywhere. I'm my own dog."

The strange brown dog introduced himself as YipYowl. He'd been born to a street dog, and had survived on his own for as many cycles as he could remember. Shep didn't have a name at the time, so YipYowl called him Bone.

"You're so skinny, you're like a bone with fur on it," YipYowl said.

YipYowl shared his garbage with Shep. After eating, they found a shallow den in the hollow of a dead tree for the night. In the morning, YipYowl began what Shep learned was his daily routine: scenting out garbage cans, looking for ones that would be good to attack in the night.

"You never eat during sun time," YipYowl explained. "There are too many humans about, and they'll come after you like rabid squirrels if they catch you messing with their cans." He showed Shep a scar on his flank from where a human had attacked him.

Shep was grateful for YipYowl's help. He had no idea how to live Outside. His whole life had been spent in cages — either the kennel or the fight cage. But YipYowl's wasn't an easy life. Shep learned that his cage had protected him from certain dangers. Sleeping in caves and hollowed-out trees meant waking with bites from rodents and bugs. And out in the wild, no one delivered even a meager bowl of stale kibble to you in the evening. Humans guarded their trash and often chased Shep and YipYowl off before they could get a sniff at the can. Some nights, they went without a meal. They'd snuffle around as the moon passed over their heads and not find a single piece of kibble.

Yet most dangerous of all were the wild dogs. Some were street dogs like YipYowl, some were pets set loose by their masters, but they were all terrible and cruel. The wild dogs attacked other dogs, stole their food and shelter. Shep had thought he'd seen the snout of the Black Dog in the fight cage, but these wild dogs taught him that he'd merely caught a glimpse of that beast.

YipYowl had managed to keep the wild dogs off his scent until one cold night. Shep and he were investigating the contents of a Car-sized trash bin outside a long, low building when they were attacked by a couple of wild dogs. These dogs were all haggard, without a trace of fear in their eyes — Shep was looking the Black Dog in the snout.

"Clear out of this can," one growled. "We're eating whatever's inside."

The other dogs didn't even wait for a reaction. They attacked YipYowl and Shep without warning. The dog who jumped onto Shep hadn't expected much of a fight; he leapt back in shock at the ferocity of Shep's defense. Shep felt like he was drowning in his rage — his mind reeled with memories of the fight cage. He slashed at whatever fur was in front of him. Lost in the fight, his claws and fangs moved without his having to think about them.

Suddenly, the air was filled with sirens and flashing lights. Shep panicked, remembering the fear smell in the fight kennel. It woke him from his fight trance, but there was nowhere for him to run. He only had time to see the bodies of the other dogs — the wild dogs and YipYowl — before a human shot him with a dart.

Shep felt his head fog over, and then all was dark. He awoke in a clean cage with a shiny white floor and metal walls.

*　　*　　*

"I was trapped in that kennel for only a few suns," Shep whimpered. "My boy took me from that place and brought me here."

"Did you kill YipYowl?" Callie woofed.

"I don't know." Shep stared out the window hole at the raging storm. He wished that it would suck him out into its fury, into oblivion.

"Is that why you're so scared of lifeblood?" Callie rested her muzzle against Shep's shoulder.

Shep glanced at her, snuggled against his side. She wasn't disgusted; she didn't abandon him, even now that she knew his deepest shame.

"Do you think I can ever make up for it?" he whimpered. "Can I ever be a good dog if I've done something so bad?"

Callie licked his jowl. "Just keep trying," she woofed. "It's all any dog can do." She looked up at the storm. "And you've changed since then. You fought off those dogs who attacked Frizzle without losing yourself to the fight. Maybe YipYowl's up there with the Silver Moon, like the way you thought the Great Wolf looked down on you. Maybe she saved a part of him, and that part sees how good a dog you are now."

Shep panted softly. "That'd be nice." He watched a swirl of rain dance in the dim light. "Maybe Frizzle's up there, too. Curled around the Silver Moon, looking down on all of us."

Callie grinned. "I can imagine Frizzle up there, nipping at the Great Wolf's scruff."

Shep sat with his friend, flank to flank, feeling the wind of the storm in his fur and the mist of raindrops on his whiskers.

"What was that?" Callie stood, sniffing the air.

Shep heard something, too. A high-pitched yip, and then growling. He stood against the window wall and peered out the hole. Shadowy forms moved amidst the shifting raindrops.

After several heartbeats, they heard Higgins yowl from on top of one of the shelves.

"They're here!" he cried. "The wild dogs have returned!"

# CHAPTER 13
## THUNDERCLAP

The howls and barks of the wild dogs soon rivaled the shriek of the storm winds. It wasn't long before Shep saw the noses of the most intrepid dogs in the wild pack sniffing at the jagged edges of the window hole, paws and bellies visible against what remained of the glass wall.

"To your places!" barked Shep.

The small dogs scrambled up Higgins's ramp-shelf. Little Oscar was lifted directly onto the second level, but the rest remained on top of the shelf with toys, brushes, and whatever else they could bite between their jaws.

Boji and Cheese stood behind the water tank, paws against the cabinet, ready to push it over. The other big dogs, led by Virgil, stood guard at the bottom of the toppled shelf to keep the wild dogs from running up it.

"Callie," Shep woofed. "You go up the ramp with the others."

"I stand with you," she barked. "We're a team."

Shep licked her wrinkled forehead. "I want us to stay a team. You lead the small dogs on top of the shelf."

Callie's tail drooped. "You sure?" she asked.

Shep wagged his tail and nipped her ear. "They need a leader, and I'm not sure Higgins is up to the task."

Callie waggled her tail, then licked Shep's nose and raced up onto the top of the shelf.

Lightning blazed, thunder boomed, and the winds spattered rain against the stone floor. The wild dogs pawed at the hole, trying to figure out how to get in now that the wooden plank had been removed.

Shep took a position in front of the hole, near the stairs toward the back of the den. He could see all the dogs from there. He chattered his teeth in anticipation, looking first up at Callie, then Boji and Cheese, then Virgil.

A wild dog came flying through the window hole. He landed with a scream, his paws sliced by the broken clear teeth on the floor.

"The floor bites!" the dog yelped.

Another dog leapt through the hole; this one sprang off the back of the first to avoid the teeth.

He landed close to the tank. "Didn't think we'd get past your little trap?" he growled.

"Now!" barked Shep.

Boji and Cheese thrust their forepaws against the tank. It wobbled, then crashed to the floor, dousing the wild dog with a wave of water and flickering things. The dog was knocked off his paws and washed back against the window wall.

Unfortunately, the water from the tank also washed away the sharp teeth on the floor.

The next wild dog leapt through the hole and discovered this turn of events. "The teeth are gone!" she bellowed.

A furious howl from Outside answered her call, and dogs began leaping into the den one after the other.

Shep closed his eyes. *Great Wolf, protect us.*

"Boji, Cheese, to the shelf!" Shep barked. "Callie! Now!"

A rain of toys and brushes fell onto the wild dogs. Those struck by the falling debris whimpered and cringed, surprised by the attack from above. But they quickly recovered. Before the small dogs could launch their second assault, some of the wild dogs were headed for the ramp-shelf.

Shep lunged into the wild pack. He snapped at whatever fur he could find and dodged the dogs' flashing teeth as he raced through the crowd forming near the window. He hoped to distract enough of them to keep their main force from attacking Virgil and the others. Then he remembered Oscar's plan.

Turning mid-stride, Shep tore into the jowl of the nearest wild dog and bounded down an aisle. Just as he'd hoped, several dogs raced after him. Springing off his hind paws, Shep vaulted over the ripped bags of kibble. The wild dogs scrambled to a halt in front of the pile.

"Food!" one girldog shrieked. She began gobbling mouthfuls of kibble.

Several other dogs came running down the aisle, having heard her cry. Soon, a large portion of the wild pack was huddled in that corner, stuffing their snouts.

Shep raced back to the window hole. The big dogs were doing their best to hold back the wild dogs, but there were just too many of them. Callie and the other small dogs tried to keep the wild pack off its guard by tossing objects first from one end of the shelf, then the other. But the wild dogs were smart. They figured out that only a small number of dogs were on top of the shelf, and that the objects they threw did little damage.

A wild dog attacked Snoop, rolling him back against the shelf. The dog bounded up the ramp-shelf.

"Daisy, watch your tail!" Shep barked.

Daisy lunged sideways. The wild dog overshot his attack and ran off the edge of the shelf, plummeting to the floor. He landed in a heap and did not get back on his paws.

*Thank the Great Wolf,* thought Shep. But the small dogs might not be so lucky with the next attack. He had to do something.

And then he saw her.

Kaz.

The black dog's shoulders loomed above the pack around her. Her furry brown eyebrows were low over her eyes, which glittered with vicious joy. The chaos of the battle, the stench of dog, the howls and cries — all the fighting seemed to give her pleasure. She was like the Black Dog made flesh for all dogs to see and fear.

But Shep was not afraid. He glanced up at Callie and the others, his packmates, and felt as brave as the Great Wolf.

"I challenge Kaz to a fight!" Shep's deep-throated bark echoed throughout the room. "One dog against one dog, for ownership of this den!"

The fighting was suddenly still. The wild pack looked toward their leader.

Shep glanced at Virgil and flicked his ears; Virgil and the other big dogs raced up the ramp-shelf and began hoisting the smaller dogs onto the second level of the den.

"It's you," Kaz growled. "I knew I'd see you again."

Shep's ears lay against his head and his hackles bristled along his spine. "If you lose, the wild dogs will leave this place and never return."

"If I lose," Kaz echoed. Her ears were up and tail flat. She didn't seem at all threatened.

"The pets will be left alone, no matter what," Shep barked. "If I die, you let them leave."

"If you die." Kaz's eyes blazed in a flash of lightning. Her fangs dripped with slobber.

Shep placed his paws firmly on the stone floor of the den. "I'm ready."

The main pack of dogs formed a ragged circle around Kaz and Shep. Some dogs remained at the kibble pile, but most were attracted to the scent of the battle. Fangs bared and hackles raised, the wild pack yipped and bayed with excitement.

Kaz panted, her jowls curled into a savage grin. "I don't think you're in much of a position to bargain," she growled. "How about, no matter what, we wild dogs do as we please?"

"We'll see about that," Shep snarled.

Kaz circled Shep, jowls quivering over her jaws. She snapped at him, first at his tail, then at his flank. Shep dodged each attack, though he sensed that she was merely toying with him. Then she feinted high, but thrust her head low, catching Shep's forepaw with her teeth. He shrieked and hopped back.

"Who's the big protector now?" Kaz barked. Her mocking tone pricked Shep like a fang.

Shep glanced up at the shelf, but all the others were gone. He was alone.

"If you yield, I'll let you go," Kaz snarled. "No sense in dying for a scraggly pack of pets."

Shep put weight on his injured paw, and pain shot through him like lightning. His life used to be filled with such pains, his body a tangle of injury. He felt the claws of fear scratch at his heart — he didn't want to die.

The wild dogs pressed closer, as if sensing his imminent defeat. And then he saw it: a pair of eyes peeking out from behind the rodent-floor railing, a wet nose catching the wall-light. He was not alone. His pack-mates were watching. And he was their only hope. He decided he had one more fight left in him.

Kaz lunged at Shep. This time he reared, slamming down onto her neck with his claws and snagging her ear with his fangs. With a jerk of his head, he tore the flesh from her skull.

The black dog didn't so much as squeal. She cocked her head to the side where her ear had once stood, then snorted. "I guess now we're even?" She licked at a trickle of lifeblood that ran down her cheek.

Shep didn't wait for her next attack. He saw her muscles tensing on the outside rear leg; she was going high. Shep ducked and rolled onto his back, snapping his jaws around the soft underskin of Kaz's neck. He locked his jaws, and, catching his paw pads on the stone, pushed off the floor. Lifeblood gushed over his snout. He released his jaws and jumped away just as Kaz's body slumped to the floor. She spat slobber, tried to rise to her paws, and slipped back to the stone.

"So this is what it's like to lose?" she grunted. Her eyes rolled slightly as she spoke. Her legs twitched, then lay still.

Shep limped to the center of the circle of dogs. Those nearest Kaz's body shuffled away from the widening pool of lifeblood; the others remained still, save for the flicking of their ears. They were nervous, Shep could scent. They were waiting to hear what he, this dog who'd been a mere pet just heartbeats before, would howl. It was the window he needed to turn the pack in his favor.

"I'm the alpha," Shep snarled, waving his muzzle at the fallen form of Kaz. "And I say the wild dogs leave this den." He bared his fangs as he barked. "Unless any of you have the fur to challenge me?" He glared into the eyes of each of the nearest dogs, and they lowered their mangy heads.

"I challenge you." The bark rang out like thunder.

A dog padded out of the crowd.

It was Zeus.

# CHAPTER 14
## THE LAST DOG FIGHT

The howls of the storm through the window hole were the only sounds in the den as Zeus padded to the center of the circle. Some wild dogs licked their jowls and panted. The few who had cowered under Shep's gaze now looked up at him, their eyes black slits, their tails flicking.

Zeus's head hung low and there was no wag in his tail. There was a gash in the fur on his shoulder.

"Please, no," Shep whimpered, the noise escaping his muzzle before he could think better of it.

Zeus's ears pricked up immediately. Every hair on his body trembled at this expression of weakness. "What?" he growled. "Do you yield?" He stepped one paw closer to Shep, his jowls trembling.

Shep regained his stance — chest out, ears alert, tail up. "I do not yield," he spat.

Shep's heart pounded inside his chest. He could not abandon the other dogs to these mongrels. But to have to fight Zeus to protect them? Kill his best friend?

Not wanting the wild pack to see his teeth chatter, Shep locked his jaws. He had to stay strong. Everything could change in a heartbeat and the entire pack would be on him.

Zeus moved a stretch closer to Shep. The whole world was reduced to that space of stone: two dogs, best friends. And only one could step out of that circle.

Shep sniffed his friend. "They attacked you?"

Zeus licked his nose. "It's their way," he growled. He began to circle Shep.

Shep shuffled on his paws, following Zeus's movements, always maintaining his stance. "You could have just walked away," Shep woofed. "Why challenge me?"

"How better to prove to the wild dogs I'm as good as they are?" Zeus spat a hard pant. "And why should you get to lead?"

"This can't be the life you want." Shep could still see a glimmer of the old Zeus in his friend's eyes. "Join me. We might have a chance," he snuffled quietly. "Together, we could get out of this."

It seemed that, for a heartbeat, Zeus considered Shep's offer. He looked around at the snarling crowd of dogs, his ears up, his tail lifted. Then he snorted loudly and bared his fangs. "I don't want to get out of this," he growled. "I want to be wild." Zeus crouched, hackles raised. "Good-bye, friend."

Shep braced his paws. "Good-bye," he woofed.

They met in midair, claws raking fur, fangs scraping jowls. Shep and Zeus had played together for long enough that they knew each other's moves before they thought them. Their claws reacted almost instinctively, meeting a flank as it whirled through the air, catching a jowl as it flapped over an open jaw. Shep would snap not at where Zeus's neck was, but where he knew it would be in two heartbeats.

The wild dogs bayed with excitement. They leapt on one another's backs and panted with anticipation as they watched the two masterful fighters.

Shep and Zeus separated after each entanglement of claws, pausing for mere heartbeats to catch their breath or to spit slobber. Then they sprang off trembling hind legs, claws extended and fangs bared. First Zeus had the upper hold and flung Shep to the floor. Then Shep attacked from below and dragged Zeus over, throwing him onto the stone.

Once again, Shep felt the sickening excitement of the fight cage. Once again, he tasted lifeblood, and it tasted good. He felt the darkness taking over. And this time, he knew it was the Black Dog. It was like the tails of dawn wagging in his mind. The Black Dog was not outside of him; it was inside, like a sickness. Winning this fight would not make him the Great Wolf; winning here would make him the Black Dog. Shep realized that that had always been his fear — all those nightmares, they all came down to this: That it was not the Great Wolf, but rather the Black Dog who ruled him.

Shep pulled away from Zeus and slid across the floor, nearly careening into the circle of wild dogs.

"We don't have to do this!" Shep bellowed. "There's another way!" Perhaps some of the dogs would listen to his bark.

Zeus's eyes were wild — the whites exposed and riddled with red lines. His hackles bristled along his spine. "I've never seen you give up," he spat.

"Why are we fighting?" Shep cried, turning to the nearest dogs. "There's enough in this den for us all!" He smelled their confusion — they looked at one another, and some whimpered. There was hope yet!

Zeus turned to the largest group of dogs. "The pet forfeits!" he howled, fangs bared. "The den is ours!"

"We're all dogs!" Shep screamed. "We're one pack!"

The wild dogs were too far gone; the Black Dog had their pack by the scruff. They began to close in. Shep felt a claw rake his chest, a fang clip his tail. He hoped Callie had found an escape, another secret back door.

A strange roar crackled Outside. All the dogs pricked their ears at the noise. Shep realized that he wasn't the only dog who'd never heard such a sound before. It was like the rush of water from the paw in the Bath, only bigger, louder. The air suddenly smelled of the beach — salt and wet and endless blue.

And then Shep saw it.

A wall of water. In it floated whole trees, Cars, bits and pieces of the entire world.

It was coming straight for them.

# CHAPTER 15
## THE DROWNED CITY

Shep had only a heartbeat to react. He leapt for the nearest shelf. Just as his paws hit the metal, the water burst through the window hole. It smashed the wall open and rushed in, snatching up the wild dogs as if they weighed nothing. Shep saw even the great bulk of Kaz carried away in the water's froth.

Zeus's head bobbed out from beneath a splintered board.

"Zeus!" Shep howled. He was a mere stretch away.

Shep jammed his hindquarters between the shelf and a pole and lashed out with his fangs. They snapped down on Zeus's paw.

"What are you doing?" howled Zeus.

Shep couldn't believe his ears. "Saving you!" Shep barked from between clenched teeth.

"I don't need to be saved," Zeus growled, and tugged back on his paw. "I can swim on my own."

"Don't be a fuzz head," Shep grunted, feeling his teeth slipping on Zeus's smooth fur. "This isn't some paddle pool in the Park!"

Zeus panted, a nasty grin on his jowls. "Always the hero," he woofed. "Some dogs just can't smell the scat until their nose is in it." He jerked on his paw again, and Shep's hold slipped even more.

"Help!" yapped Higgins.

Shep glanced at the shelf across from him. Higgins dangled from the edge of the rodent floor by a claw, then tumbled into the water.

Zeus stopped thrashing. Higgins struggled to get on top of a branch as he floated toward them in the roaring current.

"Who's it going to be, friend?" Zeus growled. "You can't save us both."

*Maybe I can save them both?* Shep reached out with a paw, but felt his hold on the shelf slipping.

"Can't make a decision?" Zeus barked. "Even when every heartbeat sends the yapper closer to his death?"

Higgins slipped off the branch and sputtered in the froth.

*Zeus is a big dog*, Shep reasoned. *And Higgins has no chance.* Zeus would make it, he could swim.

"Not much of a leader," Zeus spat. "Why did I bother challenging you?"

"I'm sorry." Shep closed his eyes and opened his jaws. *Great Wolf, protect him.*

"I knew it!" Zeus shrieked. "Some hero, King of the Yappers!" The water sucked him into the dark.

Shep closed his ears to everything except the whimper of Higgins. As the water rushed the little dog toward him, Shep sprang off the shelf and grabbed the brown yapper by the scruff.

The water dragged them both down for a heartbeat. Shep flailed with his paws, hoping to dig into something. His claws caught hold of a shelf, and Shep pulled himself up. He got his head above the raging tide and placed Higgins's bedraggled body on top of the shelf. Then, with what remained of his strength, he dragged his own body out of the salty froth.

Higgins and Shep sat together in silence. The storm's winds whipped up waves on the floodwater's surface. They lapped at the dogs' paws.

"Thank you," Higgins snuffled softly.

Shep did not answer.

"When the water struck, I was too close to the edge, watching you. I lost my grip." Higgins hung his head and lay down, muzzle between his paws. "I should have been more careful."

Shep growled quietly. It wasn't Higgins's fault he fell. And it had been Shep's choice to save him. Shep had no dog to blame for his decision but himself.

"You're welcome," Shep woofed.

As the heartbeats passed, the winds ceased to howl. The water became a calm pool, then began to sink. By nightfall, all that remained of the flood were large, brackish puddles on the floor.

The wave had torn open the clear wall of the den, and also a chunk of the rear wall where there had once stood tall doors. Now the entire space was exposed to the Outside. The rain that drizzled on the street spattered onto the den's stone floor whenever the wind gusted. It was a quiet rain, nothing like the earlier downpour — no lightning, no thunder. The storm had blown itself out.

In the dying light, Shep saw that the den was wholly changed. The wave had knocked over some of the shelves, and those that remained stood bare like white teeth. The bags of kibble were gone, as were the tanks of water, the brushes, beds, and toys. In their place, the wave had left pieces of the Outside. Strewn against the shelves were dead iguanas, palm fronds, shards of plastic, and stone. Drifts of mud and sand were piled against every obstacle that had been in the wave's path. A Car lay on its back halfway through the den's wall. A door lay on the floor beneath Shep, its golden knob intact. Scattered amidst the debris lay the broken bodies of dead dogs.

Shep could not get Zeus's muzzle out of his head: his eyes wide as he screamed, claws scratching at the water's surface, then black. Shep told himself that he'd made the right choice. Zeus was a big dog; he could have swum against the tide, while Higgins would surely have been sucked under. Shep didn't see Zeus's body on the floor. Perhaps Zeus had survived, made it to safety Outside. Perhaps, any heartbeat now, he would lope back into the den.

"Shep!"

The shrill bark echoed throughout the darkness. It was Callie. *Thank the Great Wolf, she survived.*

"I'm here!" Shep howled. "And I have Higgins!"

"Double brilliant and a pile of treats!" she yipped from somewhere above. Several other barks joined Callie's in celebration.

Higgins pawed gingerly at the shelf's edge. "How can we get down from here?" he whimpered.

Shep sniffed along the shelf. The darkness was complete inside the den — the wall-lights were gone and Outside only the moon shone, and dimly at that. Shep's nose was overwhelmed by the stench of death and salt water, and every few heartbeats the walls of the den gave off a deafening scream.

Shep stopped at the edge of the shelf nearest the stairs. "There's a palm trunk here," he woofed. He pushed on it with his paw. "It feels sturdy enough for us to walk down."

Higgins approached, reeking of fear.

"Don't worry, old timer," Shep yipped. "We're safe."

"Old timer," Higgins grumbled, sounding more like his usual cranky self. "I'm barely ten cycles old." He placed one paw on the trunk, then another, and began, belly to bark, to make his way to the floor.

Shep gave Higgins a generous lead, not wanting to trip over him halfway down. The clouds must have cleared, because the moonlight Outside was brighter. It glowed in every puddle, which lit the drowned city like lamps. When Shep finally climbed down the trunk, he could make out the silhouettes of the other dogs.

"You all made it?" Shep woofed.

He smelled Callie's approach. "Only a paw or so of water reached us on the rodent floor," she said. She nuzzled her head into his chest. "That was a brave thing you did."

"I couldn't let Higgins drown," Shep snuffled, sitting. Zeus flashed into his mind and he winced. "I wish I could have saved them both."

Callie panted, then nipped Shep's neck. "Not just Higgins, silly fur," she barked, "but standing up to the whole pack of wild dogs, defending us with your very lifeblood."

"What she means — *snort* — is we owe you the fur on our backs," Daisy yapped.

Shep panted, a smile on his jowls, and the small pack pressed closer to him.

Ginny shoved the others out of the way. "Not even Lassie could have done better," she squealed, coating Shep's whiskers in slobber.

Boji mumbled "Oh, dear" over and over as she scented out and licked clean each of Shep's wounds. Cheese stood beside her, head cocked and tail waving, muttering about how he'd never seen the likes of that fight.

Virgil approached, tail low and ears up, then lay

down at Shep's paws. "You're the bravest dog I've ever met," he woofed.

Snoop leapt over Virgil's back, his tail whipping in circles behind him. "Yeah-Shep-you're-the-most-amazing-dog-ever-I-mean-I've-seen-some-dogs-tussle-in-the-Park-but-holy-treats-you-were-just-flying-and —"

Dover nipped Snoop on the flank.

Snoop panted, grinning sheepishly, then licked his jowls. "I-just-mean-thanks-for-saving-us," he yipped.

Dover lowered his head and waved his tail as he pawed closer to Shep. "You done good," Dover woofed. "Course, we're all lucky that wave came when it did." He sat and scratched his ear.

"What do you mean, Dover?" Oscar barked fiercely. "Shep could've killed that Zeus no problem. And he would have, too, except the wave came." Oscar leapt onto a pile of mud and made a whooshing sound.

The other dogs grumbled their agreement, and Dover dropped it, but the notion gnawed at Shep like a tick. He'd been looking the Black Dog square in the snout, and he'd dropped his claws. If the wave hadn't come, he'd surely have been kibble for the wild pack, and who knows what would've happened to the others.

*But I did what was right*, he reminded himself. *I was doing what the Great Wolf did.*

Still, a chill ran down Shep's spine. He ducked out from under Ginny's fervent kisses and Boji's careful ministrations and climbed onto a wooden box brought in by the wave.

As soon as Shep retreated, Rufus, grumpy as ever, began to yap.

"It's all well and good that we survived," he yelped, "but now what? The kibble's gone. This den is full of human trash, and worse." He flicked his nose at the nearby carcass of a wild dog.

Exhaustion hit Shep like a Car. Couldn't they rest for a sun? He felt like he'd been on his paws for cycles.

Virgil growled at the squaredog. "Leave it."

"Rufus is right," barked Callie. "We can't stay here." She stood apart, scenting a pile of rubble. The walls of the den groaned as if to emphasize her point.

The dogs huddled closer together and began to whimper. "Where can we go?" "What if the wave comes back?" "What if we meet more wild dogs?" "I'm scared!" "I'm hungry!" The chorus of dogs became a single wail in Shep's ears.

"Enough!" bayed Callie. She stood on stiff legs, ears up and tail proud. "We can't let fear shake the whiskers from our snouts. We'll all be safe if we stick together."

The dogs quieted, but the fear smell remained.

Shep dragged himself to his paws. "Callie's right," he barked. "We're safer together."

The dogs calmed at the sound of Shep's bark. It was as if they needed to hear things from him, even if he was simply agreeing with Callie.

Callie approached what remained of the clear wall and scented the Outside. "The storm smell is faint, but I think we should wait for sun before we leave." She glanced at Shep and he woofed his agreement.

"We'll stay here until it's light," she barked. "Then we'll find a new den."

"And kibble?" groaned Rufus.

"And kibble," sighed Shep.

Shep allowed his body to collapse onto the smooth wood of the box. He was so tired, even his bones ached. The cool surface felt good against his side; he stretched his legs all the way to his claws, then let them flop like sticks against the wood.

Oscar scrambled up a pile of sand and crept onto the box, ears drooping and twiggy tail whipping behind him. "Can I curl next to you, Shep?" he whimpered.

Shep grunted and shifted his legs to give the pup

more room. Oscar leapt forward, pounding Shep's chest with his skull, and snuggled against his ribs.

"While we were stuck upstairs," Oscar yipped, "I was a little scared, so Callie told me the story you told her. The one about the Great Wolf and the Black Dog. At first, I didn't really get it, but I think I understand it now."

Shep closed his eyes.

"The Great Wolf," Oscar continued. "He isn't great because he has to be. He's great because he chooses to do great things, right? Like you, Shep."

Shep breathed deeply. Nothing he'd done that sun felt like greatness. He'd done the only things he could scent to be right. He'd chosen the only way that hadn't smelled of the Black Dog.

"I'm no Great Wolf," Shep groaned. "I'm just a dog, like every other mutt in this den."

"You could trounce any dog, any sun," Oscar said, nuzzling into Shep's belly fur. "That makes you a Great Wolf." He yawned.

"Fighting doesn't make you the Great Wolf," Shep woofed softly.

Oscar continued, ignoring Shep's barks. "There's still one thing I don't get," he yipped. "What happened to the Black Dog?"

Shep shifted his shoulder and licked his jowls. Again, Zeus's muzzle descending into the dark flashed before his eyes. "The old timer never told me," Shep woofed.

"Do you think he's still out there?" Oscar whimpered.

Shep panted, then licked Oscar's head. "You said I'm a Great Wolf, right? So don't worry. I can handle any Black Dog that comes your way."

Oscar wagged his tail. "Okay," he said. The pup fell into an easy, snoring sleep.

Daisy nosed her way next to Oscar, knotted tail low and knobby head tilted, asking Shep's permission to snuggle close. Ginny licked Shep's nose, then threw herself down beside his muzzle. Callie climbed onto the shelf behind him and curled against his spine. Soon, all the dogs were nestled around him, even Virgil and Cheese and the other big dogs. Surrounded by the warm fur of his packmates, Shep allowed his weary self to sleep.


Only Shep and Oscar slept. The rest watched the gaping beams where the window wall had once stood. They smelled sap bleeding from broken trees and foul gas leaking from the shattered remains of the building across the street. Moonlight shone on the scales of a rotting iguana. They heard creaking metal and shrieking insects, a weird slither and slap. They sensed that their world had been transformed, and they waited, eyes open and ears pricked, for whatever the dawn might bring.

They survived the storm . . .
but will they make it as a pack?

# THE
# PACK
## DOGS OF THE DROWNED CITY

DAYNA LORENTZ

Read on for a preview of *THE PACK*

"What are you waiting for?" Honey woofed, sticking her head Out beside Shep's.

"Shep-dog waiting to see if maybe Fuzz get eaten by snake before meet dog-pack." The cat hissed at Shep from his perch on Honey's back.

Why couldn't Fuzz have been a nice cat, a friendly cat, a cat that didn't make you want to bite his bony neck in half? There might have been some chance of convincing the others with a nice cat. With Fuzz, Shep just hoped Callie didn't eat him before he and Honey could scramble back to their den.

In the alley, the pack was moaning about sleeping arrangements.

"Are we sleeping Outside?" whined Oscar. "I don't think I can sleep Outside. Those poop bags could use their jelly strings to strangle me in my sleep!" His tail was set firmly between his legs.

"Don't be silly, pup," barked Ginny. "No dog of my breeding sleeps Outside like a common mutt." She stood and shook her fur. "Where *are* we sleeping?" she woofed to Shep as he approached. "And don't say this tottering pile of stones." She flicked her muzzle at Honey's building.

Virgil shifted on his paws. "I agree," he grunted.

Virgil paused near a second staircase, which led up to the third level. "Did any dog check up there?" he woofed to Shep.

Shep loped to the stairs. "Doesn't smell like it."

Virgil gave off an odor of nervousness.

"I'll give it a quick scent," Shep yipped. "We can do a more thorough search in the morning if I catch a whiff of any kib."

Virgil smelled relieved. "I'll take up your post here until you return," he barked.

*Decision made*, Shep noted to himself.

He padded up the creaking steps. The third-floor hall was identical to the one below, dimly lit by the same front window, but now that it was evening and Shep was alone, the place seemed much spookier.

Shep sniffed the doorframe at the top of the stairs, nearest the window. There was a strong scent of dog; one was either trapped inside the den, or had been until recently. The only problem was the splintered beam that lay between Shep and the knob.

Shep pressed the beam with his forepaw. The wood groaned, and sodden scraps of ceiling material dropped onto Shep's back. Then the whole section of wall — door and all — crumbled into the den with a crash.

Virgil barked up the stairs, "You all right?"

"I'm fine," woofed Shep, shaking flakes of wall from his snout. He coughed to clear the dust from his lungs, then sprang over the wreckage and into the den.

Everything inside smelled of salt from the wave. Mud lay thick on the floor. The dim light of the late sun filtered through the gauzy window cloths, which billowed out from broken windows. A moldering couch and cracked light-window stood at opposite ends of the room.

"Hello?" Shep woofed. "Is there a dog in here?"

A cat sprang from behind the couch, screeching like an old Car, and bolted down the den's dark hallway.

Shep sniffed the couch and confirmed that, at least before the storm, a dog had also lived in the den.

He loped into the den's food room to check if it was worth coming back up here for breakfast. It was not: The food room was a wreck. A mist of tiny flies hung over a bowl of rotting fruit on the counter. The cabinets had already been opened and scavenged, perhaps by the mangy cat. The room's outer wall had been torn away by the wave and the cold box had fallen through the floor. Shep stood on the lip of floor that remained and looked down at his packmates, who'd gathered in the street.

It struck Shep that this was the first time since he'd left his den that he found himself alone. Only the creaking of the building and the whisper of his own breath tickled his ears. The quiet felt strange, though only a few suns before, Shep had lived a solitary life with his boy. How quickly his mind had adjusted to the constant bark and banter of the pack. Then again, Shep was used to radical changes — he'd gone from fighter to wild dog to pet, from the safety of his boy's room to the violent chaos of the storm.

Shep sighed. He'd better check the remaining rooms to smell if the dog had survived, then join the others before it was completely dark.

"Fuzz said we had a visitor."

A golden girldog stood in the doorway to the den's main room. Her wispy fur was matted in places, but Shep could tell that in better times, she'd been well cared for. The scrawny cat he'd seen before sat on her back.

The girldog padded closer, her fluffy tail flapping. "You smell like a nice dog," she woofed. "I'm Honey!"

"Who's Fuzz?" Shep asked, wagging his tail.

"Fuzz is Fuzz," the cat spat in a sort of half meow, half bark.

The fur nearly sprang from Shep's back. *The cat speaks dog!* "You taught him to bark?" Shep snapped at the girldog.

"Fuzz is my friend," Honey woofed. "I know it's not supposed to be done, but I wanted to bark with him, so

I taught him a few woofs. He taught himself the rest." She grinned and waved her tail.

Shep sniffed the girldog, scenting for crazy. She'd violated the most basic code: A dog never spoke to another species, not ever. Dogs barked with dogs. Anything else was like woofing to your kibble: a sign you were four paws in the hole and going under.

Why did Honey even want to bark with the bony thing? Shep could smell maybe woofing to a fine hunting cat, but this meower looked heartbeats away from splintering like a cracked window. The cat had been hit by the storm harder than the girldog. His black fur was so matted it stuck to his skin. His spine stood like a line of hackles along his back, and his hip and shoulder bones jutted up like small ears.

"Well, I'm Shep," he said finally, "and I'm here to help you." He explained about the others, about how they'd survived the storm.

Honey listened, becoming excited as Shep barked, her tail wagging harder and harder. "Oh, Fuzzle!" she woofed. "We're saved, just like I told you!"

"How go with Shep-dog and he friends mean we saved?" the cat hissed. "You have food, Shep-dog? You have safe den to sleep?" The cat's strange slit-eyes glared at Shep.

Shep did not address the cat; he spoke only to Honey. "I won't force you to come," he said, "but you might be safer with other dogs, safe from wild dogs and the like. I can't promise anything, though."

Honey panted gently. "Don't mind Fuzzle," she woofed, glancing back at the cat and licking him on the nose. "He's a worrier. We'd love to join your pack."

*We?* "Sorry," Shep woofed, "no cats."

"Why not?" Honey asked, her head tilting.

This girldog was looking at him like he was the crazy one, but clearly she was the one who'd grown fur on her brain. "He's a *cat*," Shep barked. "A cat can't be a part of a pack of dogs."

Honey's tail drooped. "Then I can't go with you. Fuzz is declawed, defenseless. I'm his only hope until our family returns."

"Well, declawed or not, he can't be in my pack." Shep glanced down through the floor-hole at his friends. "We're tight on food as it is. No one's going to want to share their kibble with a cat."

"If that's how you feel, then I don't even *want* to be a part of your pack." Honey's tail stood high and her proud eyes glared into Shep's own, unafraid and unwavering.

The cat licked his paw, flashing Shep a scathing look.

"Some dog have honor, like Honey-friend. You, Shep-dog, no honor."

Shep growled as he considered things. Here was a big decision, and Callie wasn't around to make it. *That's good*, thought Shep. *This will show her that I can be a decider, too.*

He couldn't leave a dog alone in a wrecked den with no kibble, he just couldn't, not after everything he'd been through. But the pack would never accept a cat. Right? Cats were . . . well, not dogs. They were Others; they were strange and solitary and smelled funny. Shep had sometimes watched strays in the alley below his den, hissing and spitting and scratching and screeching — cats were weird, simple as that.

But this was one cat. A defenseless cat in need of help. And he was a scrawny thing; maybe no one would notice him.

"Fine," Shep sighed. "The cat can come, too."


Shep hesitated in the doorway. The street shimmered with heat, though the sun was low in the sky and the moon already shone like a ghost near sunrise. He smelled the pack in the alley toward sunset.

"And I don't advise we start sniffing around in another building in the dark." He then lowered his head. "If you'd like my opinion, Shep."

"What about the yard?" woofed Honey, stepping out of the shadows. "There's a little Park behind my building with a stone fence around it. We'd be Outside, but the fence might protect us from a poop bag with jelly strings. What is a poop bag with jelly strings, anyway? Sounds exciting!"

She trotted into the group, panting happily, her tail wagging, but no one looked at her — everyone stared at the cat.

Higgins coughed slightly. "Uh, miss, uh, golden mix? Yes?"

"Goldendoodle! Isn't that fun? I'm Honey the Goldendoodle! I just love my name." She flashed her bright eyes at each dog.

"Yes, dear," Higgins yapped, "but have you noticed that there's a cat sitting on your withers?"

Honey panted. "Oh, yes," she woofed. "That's Fuzz. He's a Maine coon cat. Say hello, Fuzz!"

"Hello, dog-pack," Fuzz hiss-barked.

Every single jaw and tail dropped.

"Did that cat just bark?" Daisy yipped out the side of her jowl.

Shep stepped forward. *Time to assert some big dog authority.*

"Yes," he woofed, "the cat barks. And he's joining our pack."

Jaws remained open, but now all eyes were on Shep. Callie flicked her tail to the side, indicating she wanted a private woof with him, but he ignored her. *I'm a decider*, Shep reminded himself.

"Fuzz is Honey's friend, and a special cat, as you can smell." Shep licked his jowls. "He's — well, first, he can bark. Which is unusual."

"Unusual?" yapped Ginny. "By Lassie's golden coat, it's undogly!"

Shep stood taller. "Unusual or not, he can bark, and we can understand him, which is kind of interesting, in addition to being undogly, right?" He panted lightly, looking each dog in the snout. Cheese waved his tail, and then Boji did. Dover licked his nose. Callie remained still as a rawhide chewie, eyes wide and tail low.

Shep continued, "And he can catch mice, which will help with the food problem." He glanced at Honey, who had a dubious expression on her muzzle. The pack caught whiff of Honey's uncertainty, and tails began to fall again.

Shep reasserted his stance, chest out and tail high,

ears up. "He's a pet who needs our help," he barked, loud and clear. "Why should Fuzz be treated differently than any dog we find? Are we going to turn away a pet who asks for help, even if it's not a pet we'd want under other circumstances? I don't think that's the kind of pack we are. This storm has left all kinds in need of help, and if we happen to be the ones who can help them, then I think we *should* help them."

Oscar leapt at Shep's paws. "Yeah!" he bayed. "This is what it means to be the Great Wolf! Shep even stands up for stinking cats."

The other dogs remained still. Honey grinned, her mouth open in a friendly pant, and she waved her tail. Fuzz grimaced, ears back, ready to bolt. Shep wasn't sure if he should remain strong or loosen up and wag his tail.

Dover licked his jowls. "Honey, did you say something about a yard?"

"Yes!" Shep bayed, a little too loudly. "Let's all head to the yard!"

"Okay," Honey woofed, somewhat confused. "Follow me." She trotted past Shep.

"Let's move!" snapped Shep.

The dogs — out of bewilderment? Because Shep told them to? — followed Honey down the narrow alley along the side of her building. At the back of the building was a stone wall, as she'd woofed. A metal gate hung off the wall, ripped from its fastenings by the wave. Shep swiped it with a paw and the gate clattered to the ground. The pack filed into the yard, glancing warily at Shep as they passed.

The yard was only a few stretches wide, and was littered with odd bits of trash from the storm, but one corner was sheltered by a fat, old banyan tree. Its massive trunk was surrounded by a cage of roots, which grew down from the tree's low, spreading branches. Some had walls of bark between the roots and the trunk, forming miniature dens within the shadows.

"It's perfect," Oscar woofed, marveling.

Shep watched as the pack wound its way into the sheltered dark and snuggled close to the trunk. Callie appeared at his side.

"Bold move," she woofed, her bark cold.

"I'm sorry I didn't bark with you about the cat," Shep replied, "but I thought I'd lose the pack if I stepped aside."

"I just wish you'd woofed about this rescue idea with me beforehand. I'm all for saving dogs, but now we're supposed to rescue *all* the animals we find?"

"Not all," Shep snuffled, "just those we can help."

"Which ones are those, Shep?" Callie yapped. "Are you going to make calls on whether we have anything to offer a particular ferret who squeaks for assistance? We're barely surviving as it is!" Her eyes were hard.

"Honey wouldn't come without him," Shep barked. "I didn't want to leave her behind, and I figured it's one cat, and he can bark, which makes him special, right?" Callie's eyes seemed to be softening. He woofed on, "We don't have to rescue every pet we come across. I mean, how many rodents speak dog? I'm guessing none."

Callie hung her head. "I'm not really angry about that," she grumbled. "I know what you meant. But you didn't say that — you said *every* pet who needs our help. As lead dog, you have to say only what you mean, only what you're willing to fight for with all the fur on your back."

"How do you know what a lead dog can and can't say?" Shep growled. "All you ever do is hide behind my flank."

Callie scowled, her jaw locked and ears flat against her head. "That was mean," she snuffled.

Shep sighed. Why was she making this so difficult? "I'm sorry," he grumbled. "I had to make a call up there, so I made one. I'm trying my best, Callie."

"Aren't we all," she woofed, and padded away from him into the darkness of the banyan's roots.